BAD Mermaids

Make Waves

Also by Sibéal Pounder

Witch Wars
Witch Switch

Sibéal Pounder

illustrated by
Jason Cockcroft

BLOOMSBURY
CHILDREN'S BOOKS
NEW YORK   LONDON   OXFORD   NEW DELHI   SYDNEY

BLOOMSBURY CHILDREN'S BOOKS
Bloomsbury Publishing Inc., part of Bloomsbury Publishing Plc
1385 Broadway, New York, NY 10018

BLOOMSBURY, BLOOMSBURY CHILDREN'S BOOKS, and the Diana logo
are trademarks of Bloomsbury Publishing Plc

First published in Great Britain in June 2017 by Bloomsbury Publishing Plc
First published in the United States of America in May 2018
by Bloomsbury Children's Books

Bloomsbury books may be purchased for business or promotional use. For information on
bulk purchases please contact Macmillan Corporate and Premium Sales Department at
specialmarkets@macmillan.com

Library of Congress Cataloging-in-Publication Data
Names: Pounder, Sibéal, author. | Cockcroft, Jason, illustrator.
Title: Bad mermaids make waves / by Sibéal Pounder ; illustrated by Jason Cockcroft.
Description: New York : Bloomsbury, 2018.
Summary: Mermaids Beattie, Mimi, and Zelda are summoned back from a summer on
land to save their underwater world from some seriously bad mermaids.
Identifiers: LCCN 2017034055 (print) | LCCN 2017049680 (e-book)
ISBN 978-1-68119-792-0 (hardcover) • ISBN 978-1-68119-794-4 (e-book)
Subjects: | CYAC: Mermaids—Fiction. | Kidnapping—Fiction. | Kings, queens, rulers,
etc.—Fiction. | Tabloid newspapers—Fiction. | Fantasy. | Humorous stories.
Classification: LCC PZ7.1.P68 Bad 2018 (print) | LCC PZ7.1.P68 (e-book) | DDC [Fic]—dc23
LC record available at https://lccn.loc.gov/2017034055

Typeset by RefineCatch Limited, Bungay, Suffolk
Printed and bound in the U.S.A. by Berryville Graphics Inc., Berryville, Virginia
2 4 6 8 10 9 7 5 3 1

To find out more about our authors and books visit www.bloomsbury.com and
sign up for our newsletters.

In loving memory of my granddad Paddy:
fishing buddy, comedy hero, excessive decorator
of ice creams

Merry
Mary

Anchor
Rock

Swirly shell

Lobstertown

The Lobsterdome

Crystal
Tunnel

Periwinkle
Palace

Oysterdale

The Hidden Lagoon

The Kelp Forest

Crabbyshell Highway

Hammerhead Heights

Prologue

Mermaids have been flopping all over this planet for a really long time. And yet no submarine, ship, or sinking scientist has ever discovered their whopping world.

Only mermaids know how to get to the Hidden Lagoon. Deep down beneath the waves, just past the NO LEGS BEYOND THIS POINT sign, is a small shell, and inside that shell is a keypad made of old pearly buttons. To open the gates to the Lagoon and all the cities within it, all you have to do is type in the secret code. The code that for thousands of years has kept mermaids hidden from human sight—

The unbreakable!

The UNFAKEABLE!

Ihavenolegs.

1

In a Fish Tank on Land

"May I borrow a pen, please?"

"A pen?" an excitable lady squawked, waving her arms elaborately like someone swatting at least forty flies. She tottered over to the fish tank, her large feet clad in spotted socks and squeezed into a pair of stilettos.

"Yes, please, a pen," came the tired voice from somewhere in the tank's murky water. An elegant hand, fingers adorned with pearl and crystal rings and a wrist stacked with swirly shell bracelets, flopped out of the tank.

"WE'RE COMMUNICATING!" the excitable lady wheezed with joy. She tossed a pen into the tank. "Me and you. You and me. You and your fin. Me and my socks."

There was a sigh from inside the tank.

"I heard that!" the excitable lady snapped. "I've

installed very
sensitive microphones
in that tank."

There was a deliberately
loud burp.

"*And that*," the excitable lady
groaned. "Oh, I can't wait to show you
to the world! I'll be famous. They won't
believe how I got you! NOW GIVE
THE PEN BACK." She banged on the glass
before reaching a hand in and wrenching the
pen from the mermaid's grasp. "You're *mine*
now, Arabella Cod."

"No!" Arabella Cod gasped. "I hadn't
finished!"

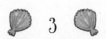 3

The excitable lady squealed as she caught a flash of pearly fin. "What did you write?!"

"Nothing," Arabella Cod said quickly. "I . . . just wanted to hold it."

The excitable lady twirled around the room, laughing uncontrollably. "WHAT A DAY!" she roared, punching the air. "ARABELLA COD, THE MERMAID QUEEN, MY PRISONER FOREVER!" A tiny crab hastily heaved itself out of the tank and scuttled quickly along behind her, carrying a sloppy lump of seaweed.

The excitable lady twirled in its direction.

It froze.

She twirled on her heel once more to face the tank, peering eagerly inside and stroking the glass affectionately. The crab took its chance and scuttled out the door.

"Don't stop until you get there!" Arabella Cod shouted after it. "I'm sure they'll figure it out! They have to . . ."

The excitable lady turned to the door. But the crab was gone.

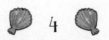

"Who on *earth* are you shouting at, you strange lump of fish?" she spat.

But Arabella Cod said nothing.

Failing to see that crab would be the biggest mistake the excitable lady ever made.

2

Crabmail!

"CRABMAIL!" Beattie roared as she slipped her feet into a pair of purple wedges and clattered out the door, letting it bang loudly behind her. Her friends Zelda and Mimi were sprawled on the sofa, napping. On a night like this! It was just like them to be dribbling and snoring away on *crabmail* night.

She raced along the promenade, the warm California breeze whipping around her plaited hair. She took it all in. The jingle of shop doors closing, the smell of hot pavement and plastic pool toys.

"Nice night for a run!" a girl called out from the little lopsided ice-cream stand that sat in front of an old, sprawling factory. Her creamy complexion was decorated with swirls of sunburn. She waved a

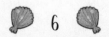

clawlike hand, bent from constantly holding ice-cream cones.

Beattie smiled and waved back as she tore along the wooden pier, each faded plank decorated with carvings and doodles—names, insults, a little crab drawing Beattie had carved on her first day there. She leaped and landed in the soft sand, plunked herself down, and pulled her skirt over her temporary knees.

It wasn't there. Not yet.

"Well, I tell you, I can't wait to get rid of these cumbersome lollipops!" Zelda said, slapping her legs and making Mimi snort. Zelda had gotten into the habit of using human words like *lollipop* to incorrectly describe stuff like legs. "And I've only had the lollipops for two weeks."

The two of them joined Beattie on the beach, sloppy hot dogs in hand. Although they were twins, they looked nothing alike. Mimi was the shorter of the two, clad in gold sandals and topped with messy hair pulled into two loose plaits.

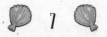

"Well, hello there, good sir," she said, nodding at a folded sun lounger.

Beattie and Zelda both stared blankly at her.

"What?" Mimi whispered. "You don't know what can hear you on land."

"Usually just the stuff with ears," Zelda whispered back, taking a big bite of her hot dog and sending a spray of mustard onto her ripped jeans.

Zelda was taller, with short, perfectly groomed hair, flicked for effect, and eyes so packed with mischief her eyelids looked like they were straining to contain it all. Her nails were short, bitten obsessively. Beattie had known them both forever and the three of them did everything together, which was why Beattie had managed to convince them to do a summer on land, with legs.

"Where's the crabmail?" Beattie said, pacing back and forth by the water's edge.

Zelda looked at Mimi, who poured some sand on her hot dog and took a bite.

"That's not what humans put on hot dogs," said Zelda.

Mimi eagerly dipped her hot dog in the sand and took another bite. "If I could, I'd tell the humans that sand is the ketchup of the sea! But then they'd know I was a mermaid, so I can't."

"Wait," Beattie said, squinting in the darkness. "There it is!"

Zelda rolled her eyes. "I've never seen someone so excited to read *Clamzine*."

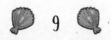

Beattie waved a hand dismissively. "It's our only link to home right now, *Zelda*. And my mom's latest adventure article will be in it!"

A crab scuttled up the beach, crookedly and with urgency, holding a chunk of seaweed carefully as though it were cradling a sloppy baby. It placed it gently on Beattie's big toe.

"Thank you, madam," she said, yanking the loose sheets of seaweed out of the slippery envelope.

CLAMZINE

The number-one mermaid news and entertainment zine!

SUNKEN SHIP, AHOY!

Belinda Shelton, the bravest mermaid this Lagoon has ever seen, is currently on her biggest adventure yet in the dangerous, human-infested Upper Realms. Read the latest diary entry from our roving travel writer.

"Today I stumbled across a rusty old sunken ship in an area that the humans call the Atlantic, but we know as Upper Realm 4, the rumored location of the hidden mermaid city of Octopolli. This is the least explored of all our upper realms.

"My morale is high. My face is freezing.

"It is the most magnificent of all the ships. I had a lot of fun playing on its bow, arms outstretched as if I was in— I don't know—a famous film. Decaying curtains hang from the windows, tin plates sit stacked in the cupboards.

"The local eels are very friendly and the water, while cold, is exceptionally calm."

=======

TOP THING TO DO IN THE AREA:

Arm wrestle an eel.*

BELINDA SAYS: A MUST SEE. Or if you prefer: A MUST SEA.

IF YOU LIKED THIS, YOU'LL LOVE: our Lagoon's very own shipwreck, the *Merry Mary*.

It was sunk and claimed by the infamous former Mermaid Queen, Mary Ruster, thousands of years ago. Unfortunately, it's probably haunted.

NEXT STOP: Upper Realm 2, the rumored location of the mermaids of the hidden Crocodile Kingdom.

*Warning: If you lose, you become property of the eel, according to Upper Realm 4 arm-wrestling laws.

Beattie hugged the *Clamzine* tightly. Sometimes she wished she and her mom were back in the Lagoon, but her mom was on one of her epic and unnecessarily dangerous adventures in the Upper Realms (which humans call oceans), and Beattie wasn't due to give up the legs for two more months.

"Wait!" Zelda said, reaching into the soggy seaweed envelope. "Oh wow, we've got a letter from the big chief herself!" She coughed, preparing to do her best impression of Arabella Cod.

"Don't do the impression," Mimi said.

"I'm doing it," Zelda insisted, in a voice so high Beattie winced.

Dear Beattie Shelton and the twins, Mimi and
*   Zelda Swish,*
It is me, Arabella Cod, Queen of the Lagoon.
*   Today marks your final day of life with legs.*
I hope this summer has been an informative
experience for you and the catering we provided
was satisfactory.

As you know, I put this summer initiative in place so every young mermaid would stop complaining that they wanted legs, swimming around singing songs about it, and just generally being insufferable. And as you know, very few mermaids have opted to keep the legs, and most choose instead to return home and embrace their fins.

Many find the experience of legs to be traumatic: there is tripping, the bizarre big toe (why is it so much bigger than the others? We may never know), and you can't outswim a shark (rest in peace, Katie Clearwater, who learned that lesson the hard way).

"Final day? But we've only been here for two weeks!" Beattie cried. "This letter is months early! How unfair."

"And that Katie Clearwater story about the shark is definitely made up . . . isn't it?" Zelda asked.

Neither of them answered, so Zelda slowly read on.

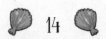

I do hope that this has now categorically confirmed in your minds that fins are the way forward. As my ancestor once said, "Finfou tabolt magegga onetup," which roughly translates as "Obviously fins are better, idiots."

I assume your families have kept in close contact with you via crabmail, so there is no need to update you in detail on what has been happening in the Lagoon. I trust that you will begin your journey home to our glorious capital, Swirlyshell, at midnight without fail. Please see directions below.

Yours leglessly,

A. Cod

Beattie picked up the letter and sniffed it. It smelled strange. She wrinkled her nose. Something was very wrong. . . . She rubbed the instructions with her finger and held it up to inspect it. Pen ink. *That* was what the smell was. Mermaids used squid ink. Beattie gawped at the stinking ink on her fingers.

"You're not going to lose your fingers too, just the toes," Mimi said.

"I know that!" Beattie said.

"Then why are you staring at your fingers and looking all distraught?" Zelda asked.

Beattie stared at the words scrawled in pen and rubbed her head, her fingers twisting in one of her plaits, making it loose and frizzy. She looked from the sea to the crabmail and back again. "This is not good. It looks just like a standard letter, one that Arabella Cod would send to every mermaid who ever does a summer on land with legs, and the instructions say to travel to the Lagoon from the pier, following a small luminous fish. And she gives us the password for the Lagoon."

"Right," Zelda said. "And that's strange because . . . ?"

Beattie held the crabmail closer to her. "Arabella Cod has crossed out the usual instructions and written new ones. The new instructions are in *pen ink*."

The three of them huddled together and read on.

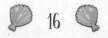

*You must enter through the secret back pipe
entrance to the Lagoon. It is of the utmost
importance that you do not draw attention to the
fact you ever left.*

    *There are BAD MERMAIDS on the loose and
you are the only ones who can stop them.*

"Bad mermaids?" Zelda laughed.
"Oh, look, she's written more," Mimi chirped.

I have been fishnapped. You must go to

A spindly line of pen ink trailed off the page. Beattie
flipped the seaweed over. "She didn't finish!"
    Zelda tutted. "*Lazy.*"

3

So Long, Legs

"And what's this?" Zelda said, pulling another couple of seaweed sheets from the envelope. "A new magazine?"

Beattie huddled close to her so she could read it, while Mimi went wandering off toward the sea, trying to strike up a conversation with a discarded straw that was blowing around the beach.

THE SCRIBBLED SQUID

We are new and newsless!

Well, aren't you just the luckiest mermaid in town, because today you are reading the first ever issue of *The Scribbled Squid*! We decided to start *The Scribbled Squid* as a rival to *Clamzine*, which is full of news and facts and nice things. Instead, we promise to write gossip and lies and things you should definitely buy. If you have a gossip, a lie, or a thing to buy, send it to us! You can reach us by crabmail at *The Scribbled Squid*, 2 Smug Street, Oysterdale, The Hidden Lagoon.

Now, our first article: **ARABELLA COD HAS UGLY ELBOWS—and is also in charge of everything, but let's not talk about that, let's only talk about her like she's a pair of elbows.**

By Parry Poach

"I hate *The Scribbled Squid* already," Beattie said, looking up from the magazine just as there was an almighty flash of light.

Mimi flopped about by the water's edge, her hair morphing from blond back to its multicolored glory, her stripy fin slapping the sand.

"It's happening! We're morphing back!" Beattie screamed as she dashed over to push Mimi into the sea before a human noticed.

"Don't worry," Zelda said, coolly scrunching up *The Scribbled Squid* and tossing it over her shoulder. "I'm sure the humans will just think she's one of those multicolored pigeon things."

"A parrot!" Beattie shouted. "You mean a *parrot*!"

The wind was picking up and the sea seemed to shake to life, the waves building and sending a frothy spray across Beattie's purple platforms, which now lay discarded on the sand, along with Zelda's scruffy sneakers and Mimi's gold sandals.

"So long, legs," Beattie spluttered as she spun madly about in the water, her view a blur of fuzzy sand and sea. She steadied herself and looked down at the long fin dangling below her. Her scales were back. Her hair glowed, no longer brown but bright purple. She shook her head from left to right and dived a little further down to where Zelda and Mimi were waiting. A luminous fish hovered in front of them.

"Well, come on, you two," Beattie said as the fish took off. "Arabella Cod said we're the *only ones* who can stop the bad mermaids. Do you think that means we're special somehow? She chose *us*, of all the millions of mermaids! Us."

"This has gone straight to your head, hasn't it?" Zelda groaned.

"Good evening," Mimi said with a bow as they shot past a shoal of tuna.

There was no evidence that fish actually understood what mermaids said, but it was considered polite to speak to them, just in case. This was outlined in

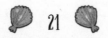

21

Arabella Cod's first book on the subject, entitled *Fish: A One-Way Conversation*, and occasionally mentioned in her second book, *Rocks: Even Less Talkative Than Fish*.

They glided down through the Upper Realms, passing a rocky canyon, clusters of glowing jellyfish parting as they went.

"Do you think there really are more secret mermaid cities hidden in the rocks, not just the ones in our Hidden Lagoon?" Beattie mused. "My mom is convinced it's true."

"Wish they did exist, then they'd have a café we could stop at on the way. I'm as thirsty as an elevator," Zelda said, lolling her head.

"Oh, oh, and I wonder if Arabella Cod announced her new SHOAL before she was fishnapped," Beattie said. "It's my favorite event."

The SHOAL was made up of the Mermaid Queen, Arabella Cod, and her four chosen mermaids, who ruled in the north, south, east, and west of the Lagoon. Swirlyshell, the capital, sat smack bang in

the middle. Every year, Arabella Cod chose different mermaids for the SHOAL, and every year, mermaids obsessively tried to guess who the four other mermaids would be.

"Well, that's something to look forward to when we get home...bad mermaids and fishnapping aside," Zelda muttered. "*Plus*, I can play shockey again!"

Shockey was the number-one mermaid sport, and Zelda was one of the Lagoon's best players.

She mimed a shockey throw and dive and then turned to Mimi, who was swimming with her eyes closed, arms outstretched.

"What *are* you doing, Mimi?"

Mimi peeked out of one eye. "Swimming."

"With your eyes closed?" Zelda said.

"It's still swimming."

Beattie snort-laughed as Mimi sailed on and smacked straight into a rare squid.

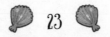

They swam for hours before Beattie spotted the sign. The sign that all mermaids knew marked the secret entrance to the Hidden Lagoon.

Carved on a rock and peppered with shells were the five famous words:

4

No Legs Beyond This Point

I'm afraid it really is no legs beyond this point. Readers are advised that unless they understand Mermaid they will not be able to read any chapters after this one. Apologies for any inconvenience caused.

5

Carp

Fintalbout mansoot belfun wattle wop senn um litlin runu fof carp! Carp! CARP! Timbuttlebot suntet belfun goort wendle ben finalot sonterbuddy finfin carp! CARP! Gottlered fishhat bramble brumble bubble no arkle fin carp. Swottle mesh tro fastlebred gree squentle squee finfon finfo tinmo binboo. Finaltleyup otter gluppletop glup ting drip finlop troplefin grunny fundlewup CARP! Suntet helfun carp ottlementlegon sandbuster castlefin wottlemot greepletea mosspot gree truuuub carp sonterbuddy wattle senn carp um. Squeefin dolptin mupple carp. Swottle, carp sentle rump olfig tyleish grup. Squee carp. Mestermantle grup olter-mag drump tap carp sottle bud. Carp, finlop troplefin grunny, you arkle starting tro get the hang fof mermaid words CARP!

6

To the Secret Entrance

Fish darted from left to right, all wearing eye-popping colors and their best scales.

"We're almost there!" Zelda cheered as she wound her way through the reams and reams of seaweed. "I'm so happy! I feel like a bread ham!"

Beattie stopped and stared at her. "Hamburger. You mean *hamburger*."

"That's what I said," Zelda insisted.

Beattie swam past the NO LEGS BEYOND THIS POINT sign and crouched by the rock shelf. Covered in shells, the shelf dropped down deeper into the sea and didn't look suspicious at all. But mermaids knew better. A little to the left, hidden in a shell less sparkly than all the others, was a keypad made of pearly buttons.

Beattie sighed at the thought of home, of gliding down into the Hidden Lagoon through the opening in the rock face, past all the sculptural shell rooftops to the bustling city streets below. But they couldn't go the normal way. They had to take the secret pipe entrance Arabella Cod had told them about in the crabmail.

"It seems very quiet down there," Zelda said loudly, lifting one of the shell peepholes.

"Shhh," Beattie whispered as she floated over, nudging Zelda out of the way so she could peep through. She could just make out some of the rooftops. It seemed darker than usual. She swiveled a little to the left to where she could see what looked like a grand, sculpted, shell-covered caterpillar. That was the Crabbyshell Highway, stretching out toward a tiny red dot in the distance, which was Lobstertown. And below, off the crystal tunnel exit, she could just make out pinpricks of lights from Oysterdale.

"The secret entrance must be down that rock face," Beattie said, pointing toward the dark depths.

"Let's just go the usual way," Zelda said. "I can't see a

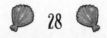

single bad mermaid down there. I can't see anyone. Now, is the code still Ihavenolegs?"

Beattie shook her head madly, her purple plaits getting stuck in her mouth, stray bits of hair floating up her nose. "But Arabella Cod said—"

"Oh, Old Coddie won't care," Zelda said, punching in the code.

The rock began to inch open, groaning as it did so. Little bubbles streamed from the gap, engulfing the three little mermaids waiting anxiously outside. It wasn't until the bubbles cleared that Beattie could see what was waiting for them. She gasped and rolled backward.

Row upon row of razor-sharp teeth.

"Piranhas?! But . . . it can't be," Beattie said, transfixed by the sight of such an impossible thing. "Piranhas are banned in the Lagoon."

Thousands of them tried to wriggle through the widening crack in the rock face. Beattie's stomach flip-flopped like a human trying to climb into a hammock as the rock split open further, groaning even more loudly than before. There was a deafening squeaking sound as

the

piranhas tried

to push through,

their jaws snapping.

"No," Beattie went on. "Piranhas are definitely banned, remember? Because one of them ate all the mermaid combs? Not that we ever really used them, although humans seem to think all we do is comb our hair. In their paintings of mermaids, we're all sitting on rocks, combing our hair and smiling, which is nonsense because no one can comb wet hair without doing the AAARGH KNOTS face. Wet hair is *really hard to comb*. And I think—"

"RUN, BEATTIE!" Zelda screamed as hundreds of the chomping things shot up high out of the crack in the rock face, scattering above their heads.

"She means swim," Mimi said, casually yanking Beattie out of the way as the piranhas came thundering toward them.

"Well, what a welcome home *this* is!" Zelda shouted.

"If only *someone* hadn't typed in the code!" Beattie said, shaking her head.

She was almost at the secret entrance, a rusty old pipe deep down the steepest side of the rock face. But the piranhas were almost at her fin.

Beattie dared to glance back.

"I think when Arabella Cod mentioned bad mermaids, she actually meant bad piranhas," Mimi said. She was rooted to the spot, holding her arms high in a fin-fu pose. Fin-fu is a little like human kung fu, only with fins.

"Mimi!" Zelda pleaded. "Don't try to fin-fu them! I really don't want to watch some piranha eating your face—it'll put me off food for life!"

Beattie wasn't listening. Everything was a blur of frightened fish, multicolored mermaid hair, and the slow and sludgy noise of the deep. It felt like everything was going in slow motion, apart from the piranhas.

"MIMI!" Zelda cried. "Oh, hamster wheels, our parents are going to kill me if they eat her . . ."

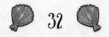

"THE CODE FOR THE SECRET PIPE ENTRANCE!" Beattie roared, desperately trying to remember Arabella Cod's crabmail. "TYPE IT IN! IT'S...FLIPPLEFLOPPLEFISH." She didn't dare take her eyes off the piranhas and Mimi, who was doing a weird single-finger chopping move and pinging them away. Beattie knew an awful lot about a lot of things, and one thing she knew for certain was that piranhas were the only creatures that would want to eat a mermaid.

"SINGLE OR DOUBLE P?" Zelda shouted.

"DOUBLE P!" Beattie roared as a piranha lunged for her. She squeezed her eyes shut, annoyed that her last words would be FLIPPLEFLOPPLEFISH DOUBLE P.

She could feel its breath on her—cold puffs filtered through rough, razored jaws.

"Weird," she heard Zelda say, followed by the ear-splitting sound of the rusty secret pipe entrance opening. She dared to peek.

The piranhas were heading back to Swirlyshell! It was as if they hadn't seen them at all! "How peculiar,"

Beattie said as a dark, mermaid-shaped figure appeared above them. "Quick," she said, hastily shoving Zelda head first into the pipe.

"OUCH, MY BRAIN!" Zelda cried as Beattie lunged for Mimi and stuffed her in there too.

"We have to go," she whispered, heaving herself into the pipe. "There's someone at the rock face."

THE SCRIBBLED SQUID

It's all about the Anti-Piranha Jacket

Mermaids, do you fear piranhas? Of course you do! Snappy little snappersons they are. But chances are, if you live in our lagoon, you'll have to get used to having them around now, and you'll probably want to avoid them and also make sure you don't die in their jaws.

That's a lot of piranha-related stuff to be thinking about every day. So with that in mind, meet the ANTI-PIRANHA JACKET! So reflective, so bright, so brash, even piranhas will want to avoid you. Tested on piranhas.*

GET YOUR ANTI-PIRANHA JACKET TODAY!

*Not yet.

7

The Mermaid with the Lobster Tail

Down in the Hidden Lagoon, a young mermaid with a large lobster tail floated with purpose along one of Swirlyshell's old rock alleyways that wove around the grand Periwinkle Palace like a maze.

Her hair was fixed in two cool buns, each decorated with little red cone-shell clips. She pulled an ornate cart covered in shells. On its roof an older mermaid with a lumpy tail was snoring loudly. The usually bustling main street, Periwinkle Boulevard, was empty, the shop signs swaying sadly, the lights switched off.

"INCOMING!" Zelda yelled as the three of them came flying out of the pipe and crashed into the cart, sending an almighty explosion of shells shooting in every direction.

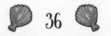

36

"MY SHELLS!" came a roar as Beattie tumbled across the pristine pearly pavement. The mermaid who had been snoring emerged from the wreckage sporting a theatrical frown. She wore a hairnet dotted with shells. "I was napping away and then this racket! I nearly shed my scales!" She wiggled her way out of the cart and surveyed the mess.

"I'm so sorry, Shelly!" the mermaid with the lobster tail said as she peeled herself off the wall and readjusted the little shell clips in her hair.

Shelly Shelby, the snorer, was the owner of Shelly Shelby's Shell Shop. It was known as the shop with the best shells and the worst name. Mermaids who said it too quickly ended up saying "Shelly Shelby's Shell Slop."

"Rachel Rocker!" Zelda cheered as she untangled her tail from Mimi's and swam eagerly over to the mermaid with the lobster tail.

Rachel Rocker was one of the coolest mermaids in all the Lagoon. She was originally from Lobstertown (hence the tail), but she'd moved to Swirlyshell with her dad, who made hats and liked to paint whales. She always wore her hair in arty buns and worked every weekend at Shelly Shelby's Shell Shop. She also happened to be ridiculously good at shockey.

"Oh, am I glad to see you!" Rachel Rocker said, lunging forward and scooping Beattie, Zelda, and Mimi into a hug. The four of them were friends, as they all lived near the palace. The twins actually lived *in* the palace. Periwinkle Palace was the most important building in all of Swirlyshell Lagoon because it was the home of Arabella Cod and all the mermaids who worked for her.

It was built by the Periwinkle family, who were eventually ousted by the Ruster dynasty, many, many years ago, when mermaids were quiet things who rarely did belly flops against rocks or burped bubbles for the fun of it. Or at least not in public, anyway.

Mimi and Zelda's parents worked as important minister mermaids—their father invented gadgets for the Mermaid Queen and was responsible for making her famous shell-studded cart and the elaborate shell armor for the dolphins that pulled it. Their mother was the Minister for Not Mermaids—she mostly had to deal with any potential human invasions.

"How was land?" Rachel Rocker asked. "How do you make the toes move?"

"What's *happened* to this place?" Beattie said, her eyes wide. She was looking up at the magnificent palace peppered with sinister clouds of squid ink and teaming with eels and piranhas.

All four of them huddled in the shadows, the eerie sound of slow swirling water and empty streets echoing in the background. There was a loud crack above their heads as the rock entrance opened again. Beattie looked up. A mermaid in an elaborate hat stalked back and forth, back and forth, up there among the swarm of piranhas. She noticed one of the piranhas was on a leash, following obediently beside the mermaid. The sparkles from the collar and lead glowed in the moonlight.

"Who *is* that?" Beattie asked.

"That," Rachel Rocker said, lowering her voice and leaning in closer, "is one seriously bad mermaid."

She handed Beattie a copy of *Clamzine*. One of the sloppy seaweed corners was folded over. "Read it," she said, not taking her eyes off the mermaid at the rock face.

CLAMZINE

By order of Ommy Pike,
Piranha Army Chief*

MAKE SHELL TOPS FOR OUR NEW QUEEN, THE SWAN, OR ELSE!

The shell sellers below will be using carts to hand out free shells in each region:

- Shelly Shelby's Shell Shop in Swirlyshell
- The Grumpy Dolphin in Lobstertown
- Shellzilla's in Hammerhead Heights
- Just Shells in Anchor Rock
- Sheltini's & Co. in Oysterdale

A SHORT HISTORY OF TRADITIONAL SHELL TOPS

In the olden days all mermaids (and the occasional sea lion and trout) wore traditional shell tops—just two shells on a string. Fashions have evolved over the years—from small clamshells and big clamshells to more experimental materials like live crabs. (That didn't end well.)

Top Three Mermaid Tops in Hidden Lagoon History

1. The rise in popularity of the Clippee cartoon meant many young mermaids started wearing T-shirts stamped with images of Clippee the lobster in a dress.

2. Tops with added chunky shell shoulder pads dominated in the last century, but are now considered ridiculous.

3. Finally, the most famous mermaid shell top on record is the Ruster Shells top, created by Mary Ruster, who also sank the *Merry Mary* ship (still in the Lagoon today). Just two shells on a string and decorated with beautiful carvings of crocodiles, the Ruster Shells were rumored to be magic but have been missing for hundreds of years.

8

Piranha Nails

"So that mermaid up there is Ommy Pike?" Beattie said as they edged cautiously along Periwinkle Boulevard and toward the palace's grand, shell-studded wall.

Rachel Rocker nodded. "But he's just the henchman, from Oysterdale—he works for a mermaid called The Swan, the new queen. It's the strangest thing. No one has seen her."

"She sounds like a disease," Zelda said. "I've got the Swans."

"Why is she called The Swan?" Beattie asked.

Rachel Rocker shrugged. "Someone told me she made it up to sound fancy. Because swans are, apparently, fancy."

"Only on the surface of the water," Mimi said

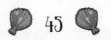

knowingly. "If they try to swim deep, they look like soggy monsters."

"Everyone is being forced to make shell tops. Day in, day out. No one knows when it'll end. It's horrible," Rachel Rocker whispered as a mermaid popped up from the window of Weedbee's the bookshop and began to sing:

"Last night I tried to glue this shell
to that one over there.
Instead I glued my eyelids shut,
which gave me quite a scare."

Beattie floated on past the Flat Crab Café. Another mermaid popped up.

"I tried to add some nice details
to make mine look less drab.
Instead I accidentally used
a very angry crab."

A crab was hanging from her armpit, looking

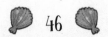

furious. Beattie bowed sympathetically and swam on past Sandberg's, the department store. A little mermaid sporting a grin popped up.

"MY SHELL TOP WAS PERFECT AND PURPLE!
AND THEN I SAT ON IT!
AND IT WASN'T ANYMORE!"

The Weedbee's mermaid leaned out of her window. "That's not in keeping with the song, Judith," she hissed.

"*We tried to make ours EXTRA BIG—*" sang a mermaid enthusiastically in the window of Sinkers! the joke shop—

"And pointy, just for fun.
But we put them on and almost died,
Because they weighed A TON!"

Rachel Rocker sighed. "You get the idea . . ."

"Why does every mermaid have to make shell tops for The Swan?" Beattie asked as they reached the palace wall.

"Who knows," Rachel Rocker said. "Maybe she just really likes shell tops."

"And no one in the palace cares that Ommy and The Swan have taken over, do they?" Zelda said.

Rachel Rocker bowed her head. "The palace is completely empty—well, apart from Ommy. I sneaked in the other day. Most mermaids aren't allowed out of their shops or houses, but me and Shelly have to take the cart around the city every day, handing out shells. I took my chance and sneaked into the palace, but I couldn't find anyone. No one knows where the palace mermaids are, and we can't just zip over to Lobstertown and look for them. The whole Lagoon is on lockdown, apart from the mermaids from Oysterdale, who are allowed to do whatever they want! They've been looting cities."

"They looted my glasses!" Shelly Shelby shouted as she lugged her broken cart over to them and swam straight into a rock.

"Life has never been better for the Oysterdale mermaids, but as for the rest of us mermaids," Rachel Rocker said, "the piranhas track our every move—in all the cities, not just Swirlyshell. You can't travel far before they catch up with you and snap until you turn back. The palace mermaids could be anywhere by now, and so could Arabella Cod. They say mermaids are sneakily searching all the cities, if and when they can, hoping they'll find her. So far, nothing in Swirlyshell. I got a secret crabmail from Klara Kunkle in Lobstertown, and they haven't found Arabella either."

Shelly Shelby threw her arms in the air. "And I have to give away my shells for FREE!"

"What's that?" Mimi asked cheerily, pointing at a locket swinging around Shelly Shelby's neck. She always wore weird human treasures. Beattie floated closer. "Ray R" was scrawled on it.

"Oh, this!" Shelly Shelby said as she seemed to melt into the floor, her shoulders jelly, her tail failing. "It's my locket for Ray Ramona. He's *dreamy*. Arabella Cod chose him to rule over Hammerhead Heights in the east."

"Oh, so she announced her new SHOAL before she was fishnapped?" Beattie asked.

"Yes!" Shelly Shelby roared. "And guess who she

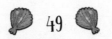

49

chose for Oysterdale? Horrible Silvia Snapp! Can you believe it? We'll never hear the end of that one. I was in her ghastly sandcastle in Oysterdale the very day Arabella Cod went missing. Silvia Snapp demanded I bring my cart over that evening, even though I told her I DON'T WORK AT THAT HOUR! But she made me go, when *Catwalk Shrimp* was on TV!"

Mermaid TVs were a lot like human TVs, only they were carved into rocks and decorated with shells. *Catwalk Shrimp* featured shrimp parading down a catwalk in weird seaweed outfits made by competing mermaids. It was full of drama, especially when one of the shrimp refused to walk down the catwalk or wear sleeves.

"I've never missed an episode," Shelly Shelby went on. "And when I got there Silvia had just come out of a hair appointment, and cod alive, is she a vile mermaid—she must've mentioned she was the new SHOAL mermaid for Oysterdale about eight times! Maybe even *nine* times! And she didn't buy even a single shell in the end. And I think—"

Rachel Rocker lunged forward, interrupting her. She grabbed Beattie's hand.

"What are you doing?!" Beattie cried, trying to pull her hand free, but Rachel Rocker had a viselike grip. She ran her finger over each of Beattie's nails.

"You don't have the mark," she finally said.

"What mark?" Beattie asked.

Rachel Rocker held up her own hands. Each nail had a little picture of a piranha stamped on it. "Every mermaid in the Lagoon is marked, and no one knows how it was done. It's impossible to escape the piranhas because of it. It's like they can trace us."

"But if we don't have the mark," Beattie began, "then the piranhas can't trace *us!* So we could do something to help."

They looked up as a cluster of piranhas started making their way back down from the rock face.

Shelly Shelby began drumming her fingers against her tail with the momentum of someone who thought time was going to run out. "Your mother is a dear friend of mine, Beattie, and she'd want me to tell you to stay safe, to hide. But I say—be like her!"

"But I'm not nearly as brave as her," Beattie mumbled.

"Go find danger! Be bold! Be bad!" Shelly Shelby went on, really getting into it. "And figure out how to stop this Swan character." She yanked a sea horse out of her top. "And take Steve. I promised your mother I'd look after him while she was away, but he's too much."

"You still have that thing?" Zelda said as the tiny sea horse curled its tail up Beattie's nostril and spun excitedly. "You know, Beattie, you always take it too far."

"Too far?" Beattie said, trying to steady Steve.

"Too far," Zelda said with a nod. "Most mermaids have a crab to help around the house, rich ones have an octopus—more arms. You? You have a talking sea horse."

"Excuse you," the sea horse said, shooting over to Zelda's face. "I thought we were all in agreement that *I* am a *miracle*."

It seemed Steve was the only sea creature on record who could speak. Beattie's mom had spent years trying to figure out why, but had yet to find an answer. She'd discovered him near the Lagoon's haunted sunken ship, the *Merry Mary*, yelling at a tuna, and had brought him back to Swirlyshell as a souvenir.

"Steve, what are you wearing?" Beattie spluttered.

It was a traditional mermaid shell top, but with pointy cone shells instead of flat ones.

"Say what you like about it, this look will be iconic one day," Steve said.

"I like it," Mimi said with a smile.

Shelly Shelby hastily plucked Steve from where he was floating and placed him in Beattie's hand, along with a pair of false teeth.

"Oh, not the false teeth!" Beattie cried. "Steve, we are not bringing the false teeth."

"Excuse you," Steve said. "That's my bedroom."

A piranha wiggled past Beattie,

Mimi, and Zelda and stopped in front of Rachel Rocker and Shelly Shelby.

"Just handing out shells," Shelly Shelby said quickly. "Take some, Beattie."

Beattie grabbed some, her hands shaking.

"The piranhas completely ignore you," Rachel Rocker said in amazement. "It's like they don't even know you're here. Oh, this is fabulous."

One of the piranhas began snapping at Rachel Rocker's hair.

"Got to go!" Shelly Shelby shouted, lugging the broken cart down an alleyway.

"I hope you can help!" Rachel Rocker called back as she disappeared around the corner.

"I HATE THIS!" Beattie cried. "Our Lagoon is RUINED. We'll never stop the bad mermaids—they have piranhas and plans!"

"Beattie!" Zelda yelled. "Stop panicking! *I'm here.* And Danger is my middle name."

"No," Mimi said. "It's Pamela."

Zelda shook her head. "Unbelievable . . ."

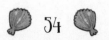

"This is a disaster. I don't even know where to begin!" Beattie said, putting her head in her hands. "We need to find Arabella Cod so she can fix this."

"I wouldn't do that, Zelda . . . ," Mimi said.

"Wouldn't do what?" Beattie said as she spun around to see what Mimi was talking about. Her mouth fell open. Zelda had wriggled her way through the grand pearl gates and was making her way to the palace!

"ZELDA!" Beattie called after her, but Zelda raised a fist.

"I'M GOING TO BE AS ANGRY AS AN ESCALATOR IF MY PARENTS AREN'T IN HERE!"

There was a loud crunching sound above. Beattie looked up and saw the rock face closing. Ommy Pike and his pet piranha, Nom, were making their way back to the palace.

Beattie thought about her mom, up there in the Upper Realms arm-wrestling eels. If she could do that, then surely Beattie could be brave and . . .

She looked at the eerie palace and gulped. "I'll go get her," she said quietly.

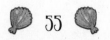 55

"Pile po sweater?" Steve said.

"NO," Beattie said, clearing her throat. *"I'LL GO GET HER."*

"Ah," Steve said with a nod. "That makes much more sense."

"You stay here, Steve." She threw the false teeth to Mimi.

"Careful with the bedroom," Steve said.

"Mimi, you stay too. If we don't come out, go and get help," Beattie said urgently as she squeezed through the gates and made for the palace.

Mimi cheerily waved goodbye. "Say hello to Old Wonky for me!"

9

Whale or Hat?

"Nothing to report from the rock face, The Swan," Ommy Pike said, thumping the desk with his fist. The small shell he was talking into bounced. Inside it was a screen showing a grainy image of a mermaid.

"Oh, that's a shame. Your piranha will go hungry now," the mermaid on the screen said. "I was sure it was a human diver. Are you *positive* it wasn't an escaped mermaid?"

Ommy Pike sighed. Up close, he was small, with wrinkly little arms and a nose with a tip that jutted upward dramatically. One eye was partially closed, due to the elaborate sculptural hat that covered almost half his face. "Like I told you, all the Lagoon mermaids are being tracked by my piranhas. They're all present and

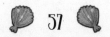

accounted for. Well, apart from that travel writer, Belinda Shelton, from *Clamzine*, but we can deal with her when she gets back—if she doesn't get eaten by an angry arm-wrestling eel first."

"I need your help," came the voice from the shell. She'd put something large on her head. "Does this hat make my head look big?"

He squinted at the shell and paused, eager to ignore the question.

"*Well*, Ommy? *Does this hat make my head look big?*" she asked again, enunciating every word slowly, like she was speaking to someone who didn't understand Mermaid. "Answer! I am The Swan!"

Ommy rubbed the shell. "Is that a whale on your head, The Swan?"

"I think so," she whispered.

"Right," Ommy said faintly. "Back to the plan. EVERYTHING WILL SOON BE YOURS! The human said she would give us the goods in one day's time. She wanted to make sure Arabella Cod didn't just die instantly in the tank. Understandable, it's very

different from the sea. It's been a day now, so you should get going and collect your prize! We need to get it as soon as possible, and I—as your Piranha Army chief—can't afford to disappear from the Lagoon. You'll go, and take Nom for protection. I'll bring him to you today."

Nom closed his eyes as if he'd just received tragic news.

"Oh, I'll just come to the palace and collect him. And I'll wear my new hat—"

"No!" Ommy squealed impatiently.

"No hat?" The Swan asked.

"No, it doesn't matter about the hat," Ommy said quickly. "But I really must insist you stay where you are and don't come to the palace. That's an order. We can't have anyone figuring out who you really are—not until the plan is complete."

"But WHY NOT?" The Swan scoffed as she readjusted her top, which was two sparkling shells on a string.

The whale flopped off her head and landed on the floor with a bang.

"I hate being stuck all the way over here, and I haven't been to Shelly Shelby's Shell Shop in days. Let's tell her to rename it. It's a silly name and it really twists up your tongue. Say it with me, Ommy. Shelly—"

"I'd rather not," Ommy said politely.

"SAY IT!"

"Shelly Shelby's Shell Slop."

"See, you said it wrong. You said *slop*, not *shop*."

"So I did," Ommy Pike said through gritted teeth. "But, just think, soon every shell in Shelly Shelby's Shell Slop will be yours."

"*SECURITY BREACH! SECURITY BREACH!*" came a robotic voice from the shell.

The Swan's image in the shell vanished and was replaced by a glowing map of the palace. A cartoon of a chomping piranha flashed in one of the rooms.

"What's this?" he said with a grin.

"WHAT'S GOING ON?" The Swan said. "I CAN'T SEE YOU."

"*SECURITY BREACH! SECURITY BREACH!*"

 60

"Don't come to the palace, wait where you are. Now I have to go," Ommy said, excitedly snapping the shell closed. "It seems *someone* has broken into the Throne Room . . ."

10

Throne Room

*T*hree minutes earlier ...

"I'm going to press it."

"Don't press it, Zelda."

"Beattie, I have to press it."

"I can't believe you pressed it."

"I can't believe I pressed it!"

"Happy now?"

"Weirdly ... *yes*."

Beattie and Zelda floated in place as five ornate thrones rose from the floor.

"*You* are a liability," Beattie said with a shake of her head as the thrones ground to a halt.

The pair of them waited, looking around and expecting a piranha to pop out and bite them at any second. Or worse, Ommy Pike.

Nothing.

It was silent but for the shell chandeliers that hung from the ceiling, tinkling as they swayed in the water.

"This is the Throne Room," Zelda said. "I'd never be allowed in here, normally!"

Beattie twirled on her tail to get a good look. It was a magnificent room with a large sea horse–embroidered rug and a pearly desk.

"That's where Arabella Cod's assistant, Marigold Seeth, sits," Zelda explained. "She organizes Arabella's clothes and her schedules and keeps everything tidy. She does the same job that Old Wonky does for my family."

Merely muttering Old Wonky's name was enough to summon him.

"Oh, cod . . . ," Zelda said as a substantial octopus came galloping into the room. Two of his crooked limbs lunged for Beattie's plaits. With a third limb he tried to grab Zelda's hair, but it was too short.

Old Wonky had always been the Swish family's octopus assistant, and he was a hair-pulling menace.

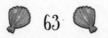

"Stop that, Old Wonky!" Zelda said, flipping her fin back and forth at him. He reluctantly let go and floated to the corner of the room, entwining his tentacles in a practically perfect swirl. Beattie thought he looked a lot like a slimy version of a human ice cream.

"Are my parents here?" Zelda demanded.

Old Wonky rocked from side to side.

"That's a no," Zelda explained to Beattie.

"Where are they?" Beattie asked.

Old Wonky hesitated.

"He only answers yes or no questions," Zelda explained, swimming closer to him.

"Were they taken against their will?"

Old Wonky rocked from side to side.

"No?" Beattie said, surprised. Surely they wouldn't have gone willingly. "Do you know where they are?"

Old Wonky rocked from side to side.

"Is everyone in the palace gone, apart from that Ommy and his piranhas?"

Old Wonky wriggled, which was a yes.

"Squids," Zelda said, clenching her fists. "We need to find out where they are."

Beattie swam over to Zelda and put a hand on her shoulder. "Maybe they're with Arabella Cod. We'll find them."

"Course we will," Zelda said, forcing a smile. "It'll be as easy as riding a squirrel."

Beattie groaned. "Humans don't ride sq—oh, never mind."

She leaned against the pearly desk. Everything about Periwinkle Palace was so elaborate and fussy. She imagined herself sitting in one of the thrones, an octopus serving her a bubbling shell shake in a pearly cup.

"Whose throne is whose?" she asked Zelda.

"Well," Zelda said, swimming around the room. "It's obvious when you look closely. If the SHOAL stands for **S**wirlyshell, **H**ammerhead Heights, **O**ysterdale, **A**nchor Rock and **L**obstertown, S.H.O.A.L., then this throne here must be—" She slapped her fin on the one that had a clump of rock anchors in various sizes arranged across its top.

"Anchor Rock!" Beattie said as Old Wonky leaped onto the throne peppered with lobster tails and studded with pearls. "Old Wonky clearly likes the Lobstertown one."

"My favorite is Ooooysterdale's," Zelda said with a pout, nestling herself in the most ridiculous looking of all the thrones—it was covered in oyster shells and sea feathers and streams of seaweed.

Beattie held her hand over her mouth to stifle a snort.

Oysterdale was a suburb of Swirlyshell. The town's motto was: YOU ARE THE BEST OR YOU ARE NOTHING TO DO WITH OYSTERDALE. And they invented accessorizing.

Zelda swam over to the Lobstertown throne and began untangling Old Wonky's tentacles from it. "*Behave*," she snapped as she tried to pry him from it.

The final two thrones were complete opposites of each other. One was covered in glittering shells more beautiful than any Beattie had ever seen before— clearly the Swirlyshell throne. And the other was stark, almost completely bare, with only two stone sculptures of hammerhead sharks perched on either arm.

"Hammerhead Heights," Beattie said quietly.

"It's where the SHOAL sit whenever they visit the palace, which is hardly ever. It's only if something goes really wrong in the Lagoon, or they're organizing a huge event; otherwise they tend to stay in their own cities," Zelda said.

There was a crunching sound. Beattie's head whipped around to face the door. *Probably just a piranha*, she thought. She placed her hand on something cold on the desk. "Wait, Zelda, what's this?"

Zelda looked at the ornate splice of crystal slate Beattie was holding. A small fish on a string was asleep on top of it.

"Oh, that's just Arabella Cod's schedule. Marigold Seeth looks after it. My dad makes those, you know. It was his idea to add the fish-on-a-string. It slaps you if you miss an appointment."

"Zelda, don't you see what this means?!" Beattie

shouted excitedly, before remembering where she was. She looked at the door. She was *positive* she'd heard something. She lowered her voice to a whisper. "Now we know what Arabella Cod was doing on the day she was fishnapped. It's evidence. A clue!"

ARABELLA COD'S SCHEDULE
The Fiftieth Day of the Year of the Eel

Morning:
Fishersize Class—fitness level 4

"Fishersize," Zelda said with a snort.

Afternoon:
1. *Meeting with Ray Ramona, Jawella's, Hammerhead Heights (1 hour)*
2. *Meeting with Silvia Snapp, Smug Street, Oysterdale (1 hour)*
3. *Meeting with Goda Gar, Eely Good Fashions, Anchor Rock (1 hour)*

"Ray Ramona," Beattie said slowly, running her finger over the letters. "He's the new SHOAL mermaid for Hammerhead Heights ... and Silvia Snapp for Oysterdale. The others must be for the other cities— Liberty Ling for Lobstertown and Goda Gar for Anchor Rock. Arabella Cod was visiting the SHOAL members the day she was fishnapped!"

Zelda shivered. The water seemed to cool, but Beattie was too thrilled to notice.

"We can use this," she said excitedly. "We can trace her steps, find out exactly *when* she was fishnapped. If we can figure that out, then we might be able to figure out *who* fishnapped her too!"

"Did you hear that?" Zelda said, swimming slowly toward Beattie as there was an almighty bang in the hallway.

"I definitely heard *that*," Beattie whispered as she and Zelda lunged behind the Oysterdale throne.

"NOM, if you eat *one more* chandelier . . ."

"Ommy," Beattie mouthed, her fin shaking as Zelda went to press the Throne Room button and hide the thrones.

"No, Zelda," Beattie whispered, frantically grabbing her friend's tail and pulling her back. "It's too risky, and it's too late now."

They huddled nervously behind the throne. "He's going to know someone was in here," Zelda whispered. "The thrones. He'll know."

"WELL, HOW VERY STRANGE," Ommy said as he sailed into the room.

Nom gnashed eagerly on the lead, pulling Ommy toward the Oysterdale throne.

Beattie froze.

The piranha edged closer, sniffing and grunting.

"Has someone been in here?" Ommy asked, running a finger over the Anchor Rock throne.

Beattie and Zelda looked at Old Wonky, their eyes wide. The old horror wriggled to signify yes!

"What a traitor," Zelda mouthed. "He couldn't lie *just once*."

"WHAT ARE YOU WOBBLING ABOUT, YOU USELESS BAG OF TENTACLES?" Ommy spat, batting Old Wonky across the room.

Beattie turned to Zelda and smiled. "He doesn't know what Old Wonky's signals are."

Zelda feigned excitement. "Oh, goody," she

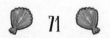

whispered. "That still doesn't help us get out of here, Beatts."

Ommy was nearly upon them.

Beattie caught a flash of his tail—it was almost translucent. He swished it from side to side in the silent room; nothing but the sound of creaking thrones and the swish of Ommy's tail could be heard.

Beattie covered her eyes. Zelda tried to paste herself against the back of the throne, as if that might camouflage her.

There was a ripping noise and a whiplike sound. Beattie dared to peek.

"NO, HE DOESN'T NEED WALKIES RIGHT NOW, YOU MULTI-LEGGED LUMP!"

There was a flurry of water and octopus legs. Beattie shook Zelda, whose head was half concealed by the gigantic pearl garland that covered the Oysterdale throne.

"Old Wonky is trying to grab Nom's lead," Beattie said as Zelda fought with the pearls. "He's giving us a chance to escape. Quick, SWIM!"

The two of them lurched up from behind the throne and shot out the window.

Beattie clutched her heart. It felt like it was trying to escape through her mouth and left eyeball. She peeked back in the window just in time to see Old Wonky let go of Nom's lead, sending Ommy flying backward.

He landed with a splat on a painting of Arabella Cod combing her hair and pulling an AAARGH KNOTS face.

Zelda dusted off her fin.

"That octopus is a joke, Nommykins," Ommy said, readjusting his hat. "But no matter how many times I tell him to leave, he just won't! He lumbers around the palace SETTING ALARMS OFF. Now, shall we sing your song?"

"That was close," Beattie panted. "At least he thought it was Old Wonky messing around in the Throne Room."

They watched Ommy nestle himself in the Lobstertown throne, his back to them.

Gently, he stroked his little pet piranha and sang, with much gusto.

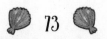

"My piranha is called Nom,
 he is funny and he's smart.
 He's really good at chomping
 but not so good at art.
He's got ninety-five little teeth in his snappy jaws
and lovely scales!
And perfect fins!
And HARDLY ANY FLAWS."

"Seriously," Zelda said. "This guy?"

THE SCRIBBLED SQUID

The Clamorado 7,
the best Clam Car ever!

Looking for a faster way to travel around the Lagoon? Want to really show off at the same time? Then stop by Gilly's Garage and pick up the Clamorado 7. State-of-the-art steering and sea-lion-proof windows, sculpted coral seats, and a shell-studded exterior so exquisite other mermaids will WANT TO BE YOU.

Costs lots.

Will probably break at some point.

BUY IT NOW!

11

Clam Car

The three mermaids and Steve crouched behind the palace's shell-studded wall.

"How was Old Wonky?" Mimi asked.

Zelda rolled her eyes. "As old and as wonky as ever."

"And our parents?" she asked hopefully.

Beattie and Zelda both looked at the floor.

"Well, that means it's more likely they've been turned into piranha food, but it's better to know these things, isn't it?"

"Unbelievable," Zelda said, staring at Mimi.

"According to Old Wonky, they left the palace willingly," Beattie said. "We just need to find out where they went. I bet we'll find them in the same place we find Arabella Cod."

"If we ever find Arabella Cod," Zelda said glumly.

"We need to retrace her movements. First, we need to go to Hammerhead Heights, just like she did on the day she was fishnapped."

"Excuse you? But . . . sharks live there," Steve said.

"It's all we have to go on. We know she went there to meet Ray Ramona. We have to track him down—figure out if he was involved." She could feel a surge of excitement rippling through her tail. "We're going to be heroes."

"Hammerhead Heights, Beattie? Are you *nuts*?" Zelda cried, her left eye twitching like it always did when she was about to say something negative. It made her look weird. "Even if Hammerhead Heights wasn't dangerous, how do we get out of here and along the Crabbyshell Highway? We don't have a clam car, the conch carts won't be running at this time, and if we try to swim, someone will surely stop us. It's illegal to swim along the Crabbyshell Highway, *remember.*"

"I swam it once," Mimi said fondly. "So many bubbles went up my nose I started speaking backward."

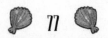

"And you got arrested," Zelda added.

"And that, yes."

Beattie slumped over. Zelda was right. It was impossible. They needed a miracle, or at the very least . . .

There was a rumbling sound, the sound of a thousand bubbles being propelled through—

"A CLAM CAR!" Beattie cried.

"Smooth," Zelda whispered. "No one will ever know we're here."

"Sorry," Beattie mouthed.

The three of them, and Steve, peered around the corner of the wall to see a very expensive-looking clamshell car waiting for the pearl gates to open. The windows were too dark to see who was inside, but the shell car looked slick, brand-new. Clearly, a mermaid with expensive taste. As it slipped through the opening gates Beattie spotted a large black 7 painted on the side.

She held her finger to her lips as the three of them rose up slowly, all the way to the top of the wall.

Three little mounds of hair—one purple, one green, and one multicolored—lined the wall like weird exotic coconuts at a fair.

The clam car flipped open.

"Uh-oh," Mimi said quietly as four chattering mermaids in enormous hats wrestled with each other to be the first out of the car.

"Please be careful with the little starfish details, darling. They are *unique*."

Beattie couldn't take her eyes off the clam car—it was the very thing they needed.

"Oysterdale mermaids," Zelda whispered, scrunching her face in disgust. "Why are they allowed to travel around without being chased by piranhas?!"

"Rachel Rocker said Ommy's from Oysterdale. They must be his friends," Beattie said.

In Oysterdale, mermaids lived in pristine sandcastles surrounded by perfectly pruned seaweed gardens, and they wore the most elaborate avant-garde hats. Some even added ridiculous extensions to their fins or over-the-top embellishments, like starfish and sea horses and thousands of strings of pearls. They loved power and anyone who had it.

"Wait a squid," Beattie said, pointing at the mermaid emerging from the car. "I know her. That's Hilma Snapp! She's Silvia Snapp's daughter."

The mermaid looked about the same age as them. She was dressed excessively, as Oysterdale mermaids always were. Her hat featured a ship carved out of rock nestled on a bed of sea feathers, and her top was covered in huge floppy bows. She was wearing gray-tinted round glasses, her beady eyes just visible.

"How do you know her?" Mimi whispered.

Hilma began impatiently swimming from left to right, her hands clasped in front of her neatly, her various bracelets and rings attracting small shoals of fish.

"HURRY UP!" Hilma shouted.

"We did a comedy class together," Beattie whispered. "At the Laughing Limpet club in Lobstertown."

"Was she funny?" Mimi asked.

Beattie thought back to Hilma swimming back and

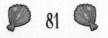

forth on the Laughing Limpet stage, the bright purple light on her as she brattily shouted, "LAUGH OR I'LL BREAK THINGS!"

"Not funny exactly, no," Beattie said.

Mimi nodded knowingly, as if that was the answer she'd expected.

A particularly grotesque fin covered in crystals flopped out of the car. It belonged to Hilma's mother, Silvia Snapp.

"Are you thinking what I'm thinking?" Zelda asked the others, staring eagerly at the car. "We could use it to—"

"I'm thinking about being the new star of the Clippee cartoon," Steve interrupted. "Is that what you're thinking?"

Clippee was the number-one cartoon in the Hidden Lagoon. As well as Clippee, the lobster in a dress, it featured Nose, his sea horse sidekick, and Clippee's evil archnemesis, a pufferfish in a curly wig called O. Steve's dream was one day to replace Nose, but it was a cartoon, so obviously he couldn't.

"It's a cartoon, Steve. And you're not a cartoon," Beattie whispered.

"Excuse you," Steve whispered back. "I'm not going to let the fact I'm not a cartoon get in the way of my dreams!"

The four Oysterdale mermaids floated eagerly toward the palace, rearranging their hats and fin embellishments. "I can't wait to see Ommy. I wonder what he'll let us loot from the palace this time?!" one of them wheezed excitedly.

"Who are the other ones?" Zelda asked.

"Well, the one with the huge crystal-covered tail is Silvia Snapp, Hilma's mom, the ruler of Oysterdale," Beattie said.

"The one with the giant pearl on his head is Parry Poach," Beattie said. "He writes *The Scribbled Squid*."

"How do you know that?" Zelda asked, impressed.

"His jacket has PARRY POACH embroidered on the back," Beattie replied.

"And the mermaid with the gloves is Trudy Strump. She owns half of Oysterdale," Mimi chipped in. "Our

mom knows her. She says she's a 'worry' for the Lagoon."

"Well, if we're going to do this, we've got to do it now!" Beattie said as she and Mimi pulled themselves over the wall and glided cautiously down to the car. Zelda hesitated.

"Scared?" Steve said, prodding her cheek with his shell top.

"OW!" Zelda cried. "Those things are sharp. And no, *obviously* I'm not scared." She swam down to the car shaking her head just as Beattie slid a finger in the little catch at the front. The top flipped open, making a loud sucking noise. Inside were a pearl-studded steering wheel and four coral seats.

"Oysterdale mermaids are SO FANCY," Zelda said, doing a mock throaty Oysterdale accent. Mimi snort-laughed, sending a spray of bubbles straight into Beattie's eye.

"We're just borrowing it," Beattie said, suddenly feeling guilty. "We'll bring it back, in one piece. But this is for the sake of the Lagoon. Isn't it?"

 84

The other two looked at each other.

"Let's get this shell on the road!" Steve said as Beattie and the others sheepishly dived in.

Beattie quickly slotted into the driver's seat and pulled the shell roof down, snapping it shut.

Zelda grabbed the false teeth from Mimi and went to stuff them down the side of one of the seats.

"Excuse you!" Steve scoffed. "My bedroom will sit in the window. I want a bedroom with a view, thank you."

Beattie fiddled with some buttons and held her breath as the shell lights came on. The car slowly began to rise. She grabbed the sides. A button flashed next to the steering wheel. Zelda reached forward and pressed it without a second thought.

"Zel—" Beattie began as the shell started bouncing out of control. Steve splatted against the windshield.

"AAAAAAAAAAAAAH!" they all yelled as Beattie frantically tried to steady the wheel, the pearly studs burning hot in her palms. She could smell burned sand.

"I'VE GOT THIS UNDER CONTROL!" she cried as they shot out the palace gates and guided the

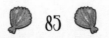

shell wonkily along the main street, through the warren of ancient alleyways, and onto the highway.

"We did it!" Zelda cheered, punching Beattie on the shoulder, nearly sending the car crashing into a wall. "Hammerhead Heights, here we come!"

The water in the highway was faster and filled with bubbles. A pair of pearl-studded windshield wipers began squeaking back and forth, making Beattie jump. She fiddled with some buttons, put the shell in cruise mode, and leaned back in the seat, watching the highway whip past.

"Would you rather be a sea lion or sea*weed*?" Mimi asked as a sea lion lolloped past. She plunked the shells they'd gotten from Shelly Shelby on her lap. "I think I'll make some shell binoculars. For spying."

Beattie leaned back in her seat and flicked through her copy of *Clamzine*. She stopped at the article about the history of shell tops. "Oh look, Mimi, the number-one mermaid top is the Clippee T-shirt you wear."

Mimi smiled as she held up shells she'd fin-fu chopped holes in. "Binoculars," she said proudly.

"The Ruster Shells," Beattie said slowly, biting her lip as she read the rest of the article.

"I know a lot about the ancient and mysterious Ruster Shells," Mimi said. "Mirabel the fin-fu master tells us stories about them all the time."

"Whoa, look at *that*!" Zelda said, grabbing Mimi's binoculars and peering through them. "The end of the Crabbyshell Highway."

Beattie looked up and watched as the bubbles cleared. Light was streaming into the tunnel. She'd never been this far east before. She pulled at the lever above her head and the Clamorado 7 sped up. They were in murky waters now. "This place gives me the creeps," she said with a shiver.

Deeper they went into the Lagoon until Beattie could see something floating up ahead.

"The kelp forest," they all whispered.

12

The Kelp Forest

In the extra-olden olden days, Hammerhead Heights was known in the Lagoon as the Capital of Crime, so the mermaids of Swirlyshell planted a kelp forest to act as a barrier between the two and keep their pristine city separate from the Hammerhead Heights mermaids, who they were convinced were up to no good.

But then Kelpskey took off and was now every mermaid's favorite drink, so the kelp forest became a trendy neighborhood of Kelpskey-makers and cafés. The kelp forest was the coolest place in all the Lagoon, although Beattie had only ever heard the stories—she had never actually seen it for herself.

"Ooh, shall we stop for a Kelpskey?" Zelda asked. "This place is cool. Plus, I'm as thirsty as a hair dryer."

Beattie guided the Clamorado 7 on and through a wall of fluffy kelp into a clearing filled with gentle light and huts made from mismatched planks of old boat wood, each suspended like swings in the streams of kelp. Discarded takeout cups of Kelpskey floated past the window. It was like a ghost town.

Mimi swayed in the back, singing the Kelpskey song, which only added to the eeriness.

> *"Keeeelpskey, Keeeeelpskey, is for aaall*
> *for meeeermaids biiig*
> *and meeeeermaids smaaaall.*
> *But not for fish."*

A ball of rolled-up kelp bounced off the window.

Beattie spun the wheel and pointed the car in the direction it had been thrown from. The three of them leaned forward in their seats.

A pretty mermaid waved at them from a nearby hut. "Psst!" She fixed Beattie with her large eyes. She'd drawn big black swirls below her eyebrows. "Pull your clam car in here. Quickly, quickly. Before the piranhas see you."

Beattie peered out at the hut—it looked nice, a little ramshackle place with cute kelp-and-shark-teeth bunting draped across the entrance. The sign above the garage-like doors said THE KELPSKEY KLUB.

Beattie turned to the others. "Should we?"

"Definitely," Zelda said, leaning over and pulling the cord by the steering wheel, sending the car lurching forward and into the hut. "They probably have Kelpskey."

"ZELDA!" Beattie cried. "STOP PULLING LEVERS AND PUSHING BUTTONS!"

Steve peeked out of the false teeth like a strange-shaped tongue. "WILL YOU PLEASE STOP SHOUTING! It's making my bedroom *chatter*."

Inside the Kelpskey Klub, mermaids with assorted tails—scales, shark, some a mix of both—chatted and laughed as if everything wasn't bleak outside. A couple

in the corner with large shark tails were plaiting each other's hair around crowns of shark teeth.

"Do you want to get eaten by piranhas?" the mermaid with the swirls under her eyebrows said as Beattie nervously emerged from the clam car. "Driving around in that stolen thing?"

"It's . . . not stolen," Beattie said, lowering her voice to a whisper. "It's *borrowed*."

"It's stolen," the mermaid said, thrusting a poster into Beattie's hand. It was stamped STOLEN above a picture of the Clamorado 7 and the promise of a special reward from Ommy for the mermaid who found it. "A piranha brought it by just moments ago."

Beattie's heart was beating in her mouth. If the kelp-forest mermaid turned them in, they were finished before they'd even begun.

"But we don't like Ommy here," the mermaid said, flashing Beattie a smile. "Telling mermaids they can't leave their cities and forcing us all to make shell tops?! How are we supposed to sell Kelpskey if we can't take it to the other cities? And how am I supposed to know how to make one of those shell tops?" She held up a bunch of shells stuck together in a clump. "No one wears those anymore around here."

"Can we have some Kelpskey?" Mimi asked.

"No time, Mimi," Beattie said, prodding her tail with her finger.

The mermaid grabbed Beattie's hand, her eyes dancing from Mimi's hands to Zelda's and back again. Beattie spotted the piranha marks on her nails.

"Extraordinary. You have no piranha marks," the mermaid said, her thin lips splitting into a spindly smile. "You can move around the Lagoon undetected? Giles!" she shouted. "Get these mermaids some of our best Kelpskey! Arialla! Come and sort out this car! We'll need to disguise it, or else some bad mermaid might notice it's the stolen one. Yule! These girls need their nails done!" She turned and beamed at the three of them. "I'm Malory Swig, and thank the cods you passed by my door."

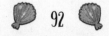

The next hour was a blur of trendy mermaids wearing shark-teeth crowns painting the clam car with cool cartoons, like a human-style sandwich (a nod to the three mermaids' time on land), a piranha, and even a piranha *in* a sandwich. They added a shell-fringe curtain to the back window so no one could see in and a special shelf, which they stocked with supplies of Kelpskey.

Beattie stashed her copy of *Clamzine* right at the back. It was a nice reminder that she and her mom were both on dangerous adventures. If her mom could do it,

so could she. Or she couldn't. She didn't want to think about it too much . . .

Mermaids whizzed by, handing them small shells filled with delicious Kelpskey jellies that you scooped out using an even smaller shell. Then Yule, a mermaid with a sculpted beard and square glasses, got to work on their nails at his tiny nail bar. Malory Swig pointed out that if Ommy or any of the Oysterdale mermaids spotted that their nails didn't have the piranha marks, they'd know there was something fishy about Beattie, Mimi, and Zelda. So Yule painted little copycat piranhas on their nails using cool pots of Sinky, the best squid-ink nail polish.

"Can I have my nails done?" Steve asked.

Yule looked at him. "You don't have nails. You're a sea horse."

"Excuse you!" Steve said. "I'm not going to let the fact I don't have nails get in the way of having my nails done!"

Zelda rolled her eyes at Beattie. "Can't believe you still have that thing."

Beattie inspected her left hand. Yule's piranha

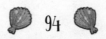

94

paintings were perfect. She watched him flick his tail back and forth as he concentrated. His tail was all shark, right down to the tip, where it was covered in multicolored, fishlike scales.

"So, what's your plan in Hammerhead Heights?" Yule asked as he finished off the piranha painting on Beattie's thumbnail.

"We're going to find Ray Ramona," Mimi said.

"*Mimi*," Zelda whispered, prodding her arm.

"You'll be great," Malory Swig said, squeezing Beattie's shoulder.

"Ray Ramona, eh?" Yule looked up. "Do you know where to find him?"

The three of them looked at each other.

"We know from Arabella Cod's schedule that she met him at Jawella's," Beattie eventually said.

Yule's beard wafted in the waves as he nodded. "It's his favorite restaurant."

"How do we find Jawella's?" Beattie asked.

Yule looked at Malory Swig and snorted with laugher. "Oh, my little fish. You can't miss it!"

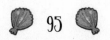 95

13

It's *You*

The side of Shelly Shelby's shell cart was hanging off and a helpful little axolotl, a sweet-looking little fish with four little legs, was helping her and Rachel Rocker pull the cart back to the shop. Arabella Cod had installed vending machines in Swirlyshell, where, for only 10 clatters, you could rent a rare axolotl for a whole hour to help with heavy lifting or moving house. They were small but surprisingly strong. And they were always smiling.

A swarm of piranhas surrounded the cart.

"What?" Shelly Shelby said. "The cart's always been like this. Nothing to see here!"

The piranhas seemed unconvinced.

"We've delivered all the shells for the day, and now we're going back to the shop," Rachel Rocker explained.

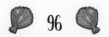

A piranha turned and snapped a shell clip from Rachel Rocker's hair, making her scream.

"Okay! Okay! We get it," Shelly Shelby said, but with a wobble in her voice. "We're almost back at the shop."

They rounded the corner, and that's when they collided with her.

"OH, NOT AGAIN!" Shelly Shelby cried as the side of the cart fell off. The axolotl carried on enthusiastically and disappeared into the distance, completely oblivious to the fact it was now only pulling the cart's handle.

Rachel Rocker turned to the mermaid they'd crashed into. She floated silently, a lace veil covering her face, her tail completely covered in shell-like armor. "Oooh, shells!" she finally squealed. "I didn't plan to stop by your shop, but your shop stopped by *me*."

"Who are you?" Rachel Rocker demanded as she began piecing the cart back together. "You'd better have permission to be out and about. The piranhas patrol Mottleton Alley all day and night, you know. Only we have permission to float freely in this area, because we hand out the shells for everyone to make the shell tops."

A group of mermaids popped up from the window of the Mottleton Alley Fin-fu Supplies Shop and opened their mouths to sing.

"NO! WE HEARD PLENTY OF SINGING ABOUT SHELL TOPS DOWN ON PERIWINKLE BOULEVARD, THANK YOU VERY MUCH!" Shelly Shelby roared.

"Oh, the piranhas won't be bothering me," the mermaid in the lace veil said dismissively.

"But they bother everyone!" Shelly said. She floated closer to the mermaid, trying to see past the lace veil. She caught a glimpse of teeth. "Who did you say you were?"

The mermaid laughed before leaning in close and whispering, "I'm The Swan."

She soared up toward the palace. "YOU'LL BE MY NEXT HAT!" she shouted at an unsuspecting stingray.

Shelly Shelby gasped. "The *Swan*."

"What did you say?" Rachel Rocker said, fixing a new shell clip to her hair.

"It's her. I know—I've seen—"

"I TOLD YOU NOT TO COME TO THE PALACE!" came Ommy's cry from one of the turrets.

"I'LL DO WHAT I WANT, BECAUSE I AM THE SWAN—AND I'M WELL HIDDEN WITH LACE AND SHELLS!" The Swan shouted back.

Shelly Shelby wiggled with excitement. "The Swan," she said with a grin. "Rachel," she whispered, pulling the little mermaid close. "We need to find Beattie and the twins. We need to get the message to them that we've seen The Swan and she wears a lace veil and covers her tail in shells! It might help. I *knew* I'd save the Lagoon! What have I always said about myself?"

"That you're the mermaid who's dressed the most dolphins?"

"The other thing," Shelly Shelby said faintly.

"Oh," Rachel Rocker said. "That nothing gets past you."

CLAMZINE

RAY RAMONA

RULER OF: Hammerhead Heights.

STYLE SIGNIFIER: His mustache with fin-shaped ends.

FAVORITE PLACE IN HAMMERHEAD HEIGHTS: Jawella's restaurant. The Chomp Chops are his favorite dish.

RAY RAMONA HAS been chosen by Arabella Cod to rule over the crime-ridden streets of Hammerhead Heights. Here's everything you need to know about him.

NAME: Ray Ramona.

TOP TIP WHEN VISITING HAMMERHEAD HEIGHTS: Don't prod the sharks.

MOST LIKELY TO SAY: "Bring me the Mega Clatter Platter with extra Chomp Chops!"

14

Hammerhead Heights

The kelp forest thinned out until there were only occasional kelp strands floating here and there. Up ahead it looked like there was nothing, but any mermaid who had ever visited Hammerhead Heights knew you had to look down to see it.

Beattie nearly crashed the Clamorado 7 into a rock when she saw the place. Deep down in a huge canyon below sat Hammerhead Heights. Tall, robust rock towers stretched up from the depths, and Beattie could make out thousands of mermaids swimming the streets—all with their trademark shark tails. Sharks of all different shapes and sizes swarmed and swam around with the mermaids, as if they were one and the same.

The car glided down, past huge billboards stamped with RAY RAMONA IS THE BOSS! and pictures of his

face. He was a portly mermaid with huge round glasses and slicked-back gray hair. His bushy mustache flicked up into a shark-fin shape on either side, and his cheeks were so rosy Beattie thought he looked a lot like the man humans called Father Christmas, if Father Christmas was the type to get a trendy haircut.

"I want that mustache," Steve said.

"You're a *sea horse*," Zelda said as Beattie stroked Steve's head.

"Excuse you! I'm not going to let the fact I can't grow facial hair get in the way of my mustache!"

"Can't believe you still have him," Zelda said, throwing Beattie a look.

A group of hammerhead sharks passed overhead, making Beattie wince.

"Sharks would never eat a mermaid, whether the mermaid was from Hammerhead Heights or not," Mimi said, peeking out from behind the shell curtain at the back of the clam car. "They consider legs a delicacy—they'd never eat a fin. They're the best things in the sea, if you ask me."

"WATCH WHERE YOU'RE GOING!" a mermaid shouted, thumping the car. She had wild gray hair and a shell backpack so large the three of them would have almost certainly fit inside it.

"Whoa!" Beattie cried as thousands of mermaids, all with different kinds of shark tails, went shooting past.

"GET OUT OF THE WAY!"

"WATCH YOUR FINS!"

"YELLING MAKES ME FEEL BETTER ABOUT MY LIFE!" came the shouts from the crowd.

The three mermaids floated in the shell car, looking at all the fins wriggling past the windows.

"It must be *exhausting* living here," Zelda said.

All the way down they spiraled, and Beattie could hear the thundering sound of shark fins and shouts growing louder and louder. The solid stone buildings seemed to groan.

"Get your *Clamzine* here! Your *Clamzine*!" yelled a mermaid with a rickety old trunk full of *Clamzines* tied around his neck. He was being guarded by a fat piranha with a single snaggletooth.

Mimi rolled down the window and stuck her head out. "Can you tell us the way to Jawella's?" she asked the *Clamzine* seller.

"Oh, very funny! You out-of-towners crack me up," he said as the piranha snapped at him, forcing him down the street.

"How rude," Beattie scoffed. "What's so funny about not knowing where Jawella's is? Are we supposed to know where a little restaurant is in a city we've never been to before?"

Just then a dark shadow fell upon them like a sinister blanket. The three of them poked their heads out of the window and looked up. Steve smooshed himself against the windshield.

"Well, that explains the Jawella's thing," he said as they watched a monstrous shark float past, covered in human-style fairy lights and a sign that flashed JAWELLA'S.

15

Inside Jawella's

They parked the clamshell car in one of the rooftop shell parking lots, next to a tethered shark wearing a saddle.

"Don't forget to bring my bedroom," Steve said, pointing his snout at the false teeth. "Someone might steal it."

Beattie reluctantly picked them up.

They all climbed out of the car and cautiously swam up to the terrifying mass floating above their heads.

The lights on the Jawella's sign flickered as they approached, but the shark barely flinched.

Beattie hovered awkwardly by the shark's eye, unsure exactly what she was supposed to do. A mermaid with a thin face and long bangs hanging over her eyes appeared. "Use the mouth!" she shouted out to Beattie, making her somersault backward. When

Beattie regained her balance and peered back through the eye the mermaid was gone.

"The mouth," Mimi said casually, whistling her way around to the front of the shark.

"We're not going *inside* the mouth, are we?" Steve asked.

"There is another way in, but that would be horrible," Mimi said.

Beattie gulped and made her way toward the shark's teeth. "Hello," she said quietly, peering through the teeth.

The mermaid with the bangs appeared in the gaps. "Table for how many?"

Beattie jumped. She looked at Mimi and Zelda. "Three, plus a sea horse?"

Steve headbutted Beattie out of the way. "Excuse you! I'm practically the same as a mermaid; I just don't have the fancy tail. Or the height. Table for four, please."

The jaws opened to reveal a long row of tables and mermaids with shark tails floating at them, picking at huge platters of food. "Table for three and a sea horse!" the mermaid shouted, ushering them inside. Everyone in the restaurant turned to look at them except for the mermaid at the very back, who was devouring a platter of jellied, seaweed-filled shells and four foam shakes.

"Ray Ramona," Beattie whispered.

The mermaid with the bangs plunked some menus down on the table. Each of the menus had shark teeth sticking out of the sides. Beattie awkwardly picked one up, trying not to scratch herself.

"Where does the name Jawella come from?" Mimi asked.

"I'm Ella," the mermaid with the bangs said. She turned and pointed at the shark's teeth. "And them's the jaws."

"I think we'll have . . . the chomp chops with sand purée to share," Zelda said, smiling and handing the menu back to Ella.

Ella plucked the rest of the menus off the table and disappeared into the kitchen.

JAWELLA'S

STARTERS

Spitty's Eel-slapped Sand Rolls—12 clatters

Deep Sea Jelly Bites—25 clatters

MAINS

Spitty's Fin Surprise—free if you dare

Chomp Chops with Sand Purée—30 clatters

Special: Clatter Platter featuring all the main

dishes and starters in a big pile—200 clatters

DESSERTS

Spitty's Sloppy Sorbet—12 clatters

Assorted Soft Sea Chunks—12 clatters

DRINKS

Spitty's Foam Shake—5 clatters

Starfish Juice—7 clatters

"Our first secret mission has begun," Beattie said, quickly glancing over at Ray Ramona.

Zelda leaned in closer. "We're crime fighters!"

Mimi shook her head. "No. Right now we're just lunch-eaters."

"Mimi's right. How do we get closer to Ray Ramona?" Beattie asked nervously. He was picking up fistfuls of food and shoving them in his mouth, crumbs floating everywhere.

"I'll just go up to him and tell him I like his mustache," Zelda said, getting up.

"Oooh," Steve said. "Yes, ask him where he got it."

"Don't be ridiculous, Zelda," Beattie hissed, pulling her back.

"Wait," said a mermaid at the table next to them. "Is that you, Zelda Swish?"

Beattie turned—the mermaid was tall with bright blue eyes and shark teeth woven through his hair.

"It is! It's Zelda Swish!" he said, waving. His arm was covered in bracelets carved with sharks and going all the way up to his armpit.

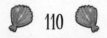

Zelda looked at him, confused.

"I'm Riley? I play shockey for the Hammerhead Heavyweights?" He pointed at his mouth. "You knocked out my tooth last year?"

"Ah!" Zelda said as Beattie watched. "Riley!"

They embraced enthusiastically, knocking a platter of food over Beattie.

"This is my friend Beattie," Zelda said as Beattie flicked the bits of food off her tail. She noticed Riley was wearing a Hammerhead Heavyweights shockey T-shirt with a picture of gigantic shark jaws gnashing down on the HH.

He flashed Beattie a sparkling smile.

"Jaaaaaaaws," Beattie said awkwardly, before she could stop herself.

"Pardon?" Riley said.

"I mean, *sorry*. Hi. Hello. I was . . . distracted by, um, your T-shirt. The jaws, I—"

"And this is Mimi, my twin," Zelda interrupted.

Beattie turned as purple as her hair, while Mimi bowed.

Steve coughed.

"And this is Steve," Zelda said begrudgingly. "Beattie's talking sea horse."

"I'm a miracle," Steve said.

"Cool! What are you doing here?" Riley asked. "And how did you get here, with all the piranhas?"

"We're here to speak to Ray Ramona about the disappearance of Arabella Cod," Mimi said.

Beattie prodded her. "Very stealth, Mimi . . ."

"Well, why didn't you say so?" he said, floating out from the table. "He's my dad. I'll introduce you!"

"Riley is Ray Ramona's son?" Beattie whispered to Zelda as they floated reluctantly toward the table. "And you didn't think to mention you knew Ray Ramona's *son* before we got here?"

"I didn't know!" Zelda said. "I hardly know Riley. I've only played shockey with him a couple of times. And knocked his teeth out."

Steve shot past them and dived into Ray Ramona's bushy mustache.

"I look good in a mustache, don't I?" Steve shouted. "Oooh, and it's *warm*."

Riley Ramona introduced them all—except for Steve, who was lost somewhere inside Ray Ramona's mustache.

"They're here to speak to you about the disappearance of Arabella Cod," Riley explained.

"Arabella Cod, you say?" Ray Ramona said, twirling his mustache. "Tell me one thing first. How were you able to get all the way here from Swirlyshell without alerting the piranhas?"

Beattie and Zelda looked at each other. Mimi enthusiastically devoured a chomp chop, a sand-covered jellied lump that wiggled excessively.

"We, um—" Beattie began.

"The piranhas can't trace us," Mimi said through a mouthful of food. "Because we were on land doing a summer with legs when Ommy did the thing with

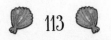

the nails." She held up her hand. "These are fake piranha nails."

Zelda slapped Mimi's fin under the table.

Beattie put her head in her hands. All their secrets, spilled out on the table like a Clatter Platter. Perhaps Ray Ramona was in on it and he'd capture them. Turn them into one gigantic chomp chop. She felt sick.

"*Really*," Ray Ramona said, his eyes wide. He reached across the table for a chomp chop. Beattie jumped. "Well then, it's just you and the Oysterdale mermaids who can move freely around the Lagoon. Ommy lets those Oysterdale mermaids do anything. The rest of us are stuck. The chomp chops are running low, there are curfews, and everyone's so busy making these shell tops, the city is slowly grinding to a standstill!" He slapped the table, making the plates rattle.

The restaurant fell silent.

He looked sheepishly at his fist. "And I'm powerless to stop it. All I'm good for these days is hiding out in this old shark."

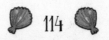

Ella poked her head out from the kitchen. "Five star-fish rating, this old shark has. Don't you forget it."

Beattie unfurled her tense tail a little under the table. Ray Ramona didn't seem to be in on it, or if he was, he was hiding it well. Surely someone who had a son as friendly as Riley couldn't be bad . . .

"We travel in the Bad Mermaid Mobile and we mean business," Zelda said, trying to sound cool. "No piranha can mess with us. We're going to save the Lagoon." She sipped her drink and then spat it out all over the table. "BLEUGH, WHAT'S IN THAT FOAM SHAKE?"

"That's not a foam shake, that's crab cream," Riley said.

"I knew that . . . ," Zelda lied.

"You met Arabella Cod here on the very day she went missing. Where is she?" Beattie interrupted.

Ray Ramona looked into his crab cream, his face suddenly fraught, his trademark mustache framing a sad frown. "We did meet. We had lunch right here, for one hour, and then she headed to Oysterdale for her meeting with Silvia Snapp. She sees everyone in the

SHOAL in order. H. O. A. L. Hammerhead Heights, then Oysterdale, then Anchor Rock, then Lobstertown."

Beattie leaned back in her seat and studied Ray Ramona. He seemed to be telling the truth.

"We've been searching for her around Hammerhead Heights," Riley said, "whenever we get a chance to sneak out of Jawella's. Not a single mermaid in Hammerhead Heights has found her."

"What do you think happened to her?" Zelda asked.

Ray Ramona looked awkwardly around the restaurant. "You kids don't know what you're taking on. There's a rumor of powerful magic, old magic, *dark* magic." He held up his piranha-stamped nails. "But the piranhas don't trace you, so maybe that means you have a chance . . ."

He fiddled with his mustache, curling it so much the left side no longer resembled a fish fin but was just a clump of messy hair. Steve floated out of it, looking dizzy.

"Excuse you!"

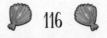

"That sea horse is talking," Ray Ramona spluttered.

"I know," Steve said, floating onto Beattie's shoulder. "I'm a miracle."

"What do you know about Arabella Cod's fishnapping?" Beattie pressed.

"From what I've heard, she reached Oysterdale and met with Silvia Snapp," he explained. "She was supposed to meet Goda Gar in Anchor Rock next, but according to my spy sharks, Goda Gar says she never arrived."

"You have sharks that spy?" Beattie asked.

"We have sharks that do everything. You're sitting in one that's a *restaurant*," Ray Ramona said with a wink. "Still haven't figured out who The Swan is or why we all have to make shell tops," he added.

Beattie nodded. "We're hoping we can find Arabella Cod and then she'll fix everything, like she always does."

Ray Ramona leaned in closer, like he'd been itching to talk to someone about it.

He unrolled a large map of the Lagoon, sweeping Clatter Platter plates onto the floor. "Arabella Cod was here," he said pointing at Oysterdale on the map. "And then she was gone."

Beattie studied the map carefully.

"I think Silvia Snapp of Oysterdale did it," Ray Ramona whispered. "The Oysterdale mermaids are friends with Ommy. They visit him in the palace. It's like he owes them something. They are the only mermaids who aren't controlled by the piranhas, they can do whatever they want—one of them even came here the other day and took a baby shark, said she was going to make it into a live handbag. I hope it ate her lipstick."

"And where were you all afternoon the day Arabella Cod vanished?" Mimi asked.

"I was here," Ray Ramona said as Ella plunked more chomp chops down on the table. "Wasn't I, Ella?"

"You were—all day. He's always here."

Ray Ramona leaned in closer. "The thing is, it would be impossible to get near Arabella Cod. Her royal, shell-studded carriage is robust, and the dolphins that pull it are lethal and always guard her. Whoever fishnapped her must've locked up her dolphins too. And it must be somewhere secure—because as soon as they got free, they'd shoot off to find her, and nothing would stop them."

"But where would you hide Arabella Cod, a palace full of mermaids, *and* some lethal dolphins?" Beattie pondered.

"That's the big question," Riley said.

"But what we do know," Ray Ramona said, "is that the day Arabella Cod went missing was marked for official SHOAL business, which means the dolphins would've only let four mermaids near her—the four mermaids in the SHOAL."

"So there are only four mermaids who could have done it?" Beattie asked.

Ray Ramona nodded as Riley threw a copy of *Clamzine* across the table to Beattie, one seaweed page folded down neatly at the corner.

CLAMZINE

LIBERTY LING, LEADER OF LOBSTERTOWN, SAYS ALL-AFTERNOON SHOCKEY MATCH WAS A SUCCESS

THE MATCH WAS a glorious riot from start to finish, giving Liberty Ling plenty of time to show off her moves. And at the 3 p.m. halftime, Trout and Pout performed their most famous and popular song, "Flop, Flop, Bang!" Liberty Ling scored a whopping 104 points in the first half and only 2 points in the second half.

The shockey match was unfortunately overshadowed by the events later that day, when Arabella Cod VANISHED.

"So we can rule out Liberty Ling," Riley said. "She was playing shockey when Arabella Cod vanished."

"And you can rule me out," Ray Ramona said. "I've got my alibi. I was here in Jawella's."

Beattie took the *Clamzine* and tucked it into her tail. "That leaves Silvia Snapp and Goda Gar. We'll check out Silvia Snapp first, see if she met with Arabella Cod."

"You'll know if she did," Ray Ramona said.

"How?" Beattie whispered.

He held up a chubby palm to reveal a shell-shaped stamp on his skin. He rubbed it. "Permanent," he said. "Until you are no longer in the SHOAL. She stamps everyone from the SHOAL when she meets them officially for the first time."

"So if Silvia Snapp has the stamp . . . ," Beattie began.

"Then she saw Arabella Cod," Ray Ramona said, picking up a chomp chop and biting into it. "But what you have to figure out is, did Arabella Cod ever leave Oysterdale? Or did Silvia Snapp *fishnap* her?"

16

Crime

Jawella's disappeared into the distance. The mermaids waved as Ray and Riley Ramona sailed off in the shark's jaws.

"Well, they were very nice," Beattie said as they swam back to the roof, where they'd parked the Clamorado 7. In a nearby window Beattie could see a mermaid having a seaweed bath and humming to herself—the tune dancing out the window and bouncing around the empty alleys between the buildings.

Beattie stopped. Her heart lurched. She could see something in the clam car!

Something mermaid-shaped.

"Hey!" she cried, racing toward it.

"BEATTIE!" Zelda and Mimi called after her. "WAIT!"

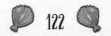

The car took off, whooshing past Beattie—the mermaid at the wheel had a squid-ink mask painted across his eyes, like a human burglar.

"NOOOOOOOOO!" Beattie roared. "WE NEED TO GIVE THAT BACK!" She thought about chasing after him, but she'd never catch up, the clam car was too fast. She turned and looked at the shark with the saddle still tethered on the roof.

"BEATTIE! WHAT ARE YOU DOING?" she heard Zelda cry as she shot off on the shark, bouncing about in the saddle like a dancing jellyfish.

"Whuwhuwhuwhu!" she yelled, her whole face vibrating as the shark charged on. She tried pulling on the reins but it sent the shark spinning upside down. "Right side up!" she cried. "Right side up!"

The clam car was up ahead, weaving in and out of the tower blocks.

"GET THAT CLAM CAR!" Beattie cried, pulling the loose reins left and right, unsure if it was actually doing anything. She ducked and dived as the shark bent this way and that, weaving through the tower blocks like a pro.

The clam car took a sharp right and sailed through a window.

There was a scream. "GET THAT CLAM CAR OUT OF MY KITCHEN!" came a cry from the mermaid inside.

Beattie trundled through with the shark.

"AND THE SHARK!" the mermaid roared.

Beattie leaned forward in the saddle, getting her balance for the first time. She was gaining on the clam car! Closer and closer she got. She didn't know if it would work but she found herself saying, "Bite it!"

The shark lunged and snapped down. The clam car shot forward.

"AGAIN!" Beattie cried, squeezing her eyes closed as the shark lunged and CRUNCHED!

She opened her eyes just in time to see the robber mermaid shoot out of the car and down an alleyway.

"I WON! I BEAT CRIME!" Beattie yelled, brandishing a fist. She dismounted the shark, throwing the reins over its back and giving it a big pat on the neck. "Oh no," she said, looking guiltily at the shark she'd stolen. "I've done a crime . . . We'll just, um, drop you off back at that rooftop where we found you on our way out of here."

Zelda and Mimi came swimming overhead. "There she is!" Mimi cried. "Down there, and she's got the clam car!"

As they came closer Beattie could see Steve was hyperventilating on Mimi's shoulder.

"Never. Do. That. Again. You. Are. My. World. Beattie."

Beattie plucked him off Mimi's shoulder and rubbed her nose against his.

"What a hero," Zelda said, playfully punching her.

Beattie tied the shark to the car and jumped inside, grabbing the steering wheel, her fingers with their piranha-print nails wrapped tightly around it. "To Oysterdale!" she said confidently.

But none of them noticed what all the chasing and bashing had done to the side of the clam car. The painting of a piranha in a sandwich had flaked off, revealing the iconic 7 of the Clamorado.

CLAMZINE

SILVIA SNAPP

SILVIA SNAPP HAS been chosen to rule over Oysterdale, the sandcastle-filled suburb known to produce some of the most elaborate and irritating mermaids in the Lagoon. Here's what you need to know about her.

NAME: Silvia Snapp.

RULER OF: Oysterdale.

STYLE SIGNIFIER: "My expensive and elaborately sculpted Hipplebee hats. I never leave home without one on my head."

FAVORITE PLACE IN OYSTERDALE: "Curly Clips, the hairdresser—they have a dive-thru service if you're in a rush. The four-hour Electric Eel treatment is my favorite. It makes my hair HUGE."

TOP TIP WHEN VISITING OYSTERDALE: If you're not the best at absolutely everything, then they won't let you in.

MOST LIKELY TO SAY: "Get off my perfectly pruned seaweed lawn, you stupid sea snail!" (Oysterdale is currently struggling with a sea-snail infestation.)

17

The Ommy Show!

The clam car pushed on back through the kelp forest, and before long the scenery shifted to murky expanses, little clusters of coral reef, and the magnificent spires of Swirlyshell in the distance. They'd have to enter the city, then take the crystal-covered tunnel to Oysterdale.

Oysterdale was surrounded by a large crystal wall that rose up high, all the way to the rock entrance, like a fortress separating it from the rest of Swirlyshell. That's the way the Oysterdale mermaids liked it.

The entrance to the tunnel was next to Swirlyshell's oldest and grandest hotel, The Queen Conch. The tunnel entrance was framed with low-hanging crystals and a pearl sign that read TO OYSTERDALE (WHERE ACCESSORIZING FINS WAS INVENTED).

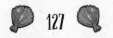

Beattie parked the clam car behind the hotel's sculpted coral hedge, and the three of them got out and sneakily peered through the gaps.

"Something's going on," Zelda said.

Streams of excited Oysterdale mermaids—wearing ghastly hats and chattering loudly over each other—were filing into the Oysterdale tunnel, some in clam cars, some on octopus. They were carrying huge bags and shell trunks crammed with goodies.

"They've been looting Swirlyshell!" Beattie cried. "I can't *believe* Ommy's let them do that."

An octopus in the middle of the pack started bucking, its diamond-studded tentacles flailing. Its rider went flying—straight into a mermaid with an armful of seaweed flyers, sending them scattering everywhere. Beattie slipped her hand underneath the coral hedge they were hiding behind and grabbed one.

THE SCRIBBLED SQUID

Roll up, roll up!

Get your fabulous fins to the
OMMY SHOW! A tribute to our palace-dwelling
friend, but not including him as he is very busy being
the Piranha Army chief.

The show will feature songs, dancing, and thousands
of sea creatures all dressed to look like Ommy,
which might look excellent or terrifying.
We'll soon see.

Only Oysterdale mermaids are invited. The rest of
you can just sit at home being jealous.

Beattie grinned. "We'll sneak into Oysterdale while they're all at the Ommy Show and have a good look around Silvia Snapp's house."

"SANDWICH! SEVEN! SANDWICH! SEVEN!" Steve cried.

The three of them spun around.

"I wish he had an off button," Zelda groaned.

Steve was pinging off the car repeatedly, hitting the part where the paint had flaked off and making it worse.

"Oh no," Beattie said, trying not to panic. "The piranha in a sandwich is gone. The 7 is visible again!"

"There are probably a million Clamorado 7s in Oysterdale," Zelda said. "They won't notice."

"You hope," Mimi said.

"I know," Beattie said, thinking fast. "We'll hide the car down a side street in Oysterdale, near the tunnel entrance, and then swim to Silvia Snapp's house. That's safer. We can't park the car we stole from her outside her house . . ." She slapped the Ommy Show flyer over the 7. "And that'll keep it covered . . . probably."

Beattie steered the car sharply to the left as they emerged from the crystal tunnel and pulled onto a dark little side street near the Oysterdale Theater.

"I'm going to have a quick look at the Ommy Show," Zelda said, pulling herself out of the clam car and heading toward the side of the theater.

Beattie watched in horror as she slipped in through a side entrance.

"Not *again*, Zelda," she said with a sigh, darting after her. "She'd better not press any buttons."

The theater was perfectly round, with huge shell curtains and ample pearl-studded bench seats and boxes.

"It looks like the show is about to start," Zelda whispered excitedly. "I bet it's awful."

They were huddled under a row of seats. The elaborately adorned fins of the Oysterdale mermaids sitting above them flapped in their faces.

The lights dimmed.

The crowd fell silent.

"I'm bored already," Steve whispered.

A bunch of pufferfish with Ommy-style hats burst onto the stage, launching themselves up high and forming spectacular patterns. Like slimy fireworks with eyes.

"Let's go," Beattie said, glancing around her. They were hidden, but a mermaid with a good pair of shell binoculars would be able to see them from the other side of the theater. And plenty of the mermaids had shell binoculars poised for the tiny tap-dancing sea worms.

"Not *yet*," Zelda insisted. "It's just getting good!"

"Is it?" Steve said as a starfish exploded and little shrimp scattered across the stage in dubious formation.

"The shrimp are impressive," Mimi said as a whale in a hat landed with an almighty thud on top of the poor things. "And also squashed," she added as the crowd awkwardly clapped, unsure if it was the end of the first performance or just an unfortunate accident.

The music from the orchestra of mermaids picked up, getting louder and more sinister by the second. Beattie shivered and shot Zelda a look.

"All right, all right," Zelda moaned as they stealthily floated out of the theater.

"Now then." Beattie smiled pointedly. "Arabella Cod's schedule said she was meeting Silvia Snapp on Smug Street. That must be where she lives."

"What number do you think it is?" Steve asked.

"Number one," Mimi said.

"Of course!" Beattie smiled. "The best number. Why didn't I think of that?"

And so, off they went, down the street and around the bend, until they saw the sign for SMUG STREET, in bright glittery letters.

"This is going to be a piece of doughnut," Zelda said,

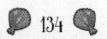

putting her arms around Beattie and Mimi as they headed toward the biggest sandcastle on the street. "Piece. Of. Doughnut."

But they weren't alone.

18

Sandcastles

"Wow," Beattie said as she glanced up and down Smug Street. It was filled with sandcastles—enormous ones with crystal windows—and surrounded by perfectly carved crystal fences, smooth seaweed lawns, and little pots of sea flowers.

The three of them floated outside the door to number one. The door itself wasn't really a door at all but rather a giant pair of fake fish lips covered in crystals.

Steve pondered it for a moment. "Bit much," he decided.

Beattie floated up to the lips and prodded them. They were solid but seemed to move. "I think it's open. We can just squeeze in," she whispered, pushing an arm through.

Emerging at the other side of the fish lips, they made their way down a long corridor with crystal ornaments and pearl trinkets propped up on either side. It was like crawling inside a treasure chest that was constantly vomiting itself up, over and over again.

Every trickle of water, every creak or falling grain of sand made Beattie jump.

"This looks promising," Zelda said, poking her head through one of the great sand arches into a room crammed with bookcases.

Beattie did a loop of the room. It smelled of sweetened kelp and damp sand, and she could feel in her tailbones that they were onto something. She began rifling through crystal drawers and seaweed scripts, looking for anything sinister, anything about Arabella Cod. There was nothing, just receipts for shells and hairdos at Curly Clips.

Zelda flicked through the latest issue of *Clamzine*. "Look, it's got profiles of all the SHOAL mermaids. Might be useful," she said, stuffing it in the inside pocket of her waistcoat.

"OPEN, FISH LIPS!" they heard a mermaid shout.

Beattie spun around, her eyes wide.

"That's Hilma Snapp," she hissed as Zelda and Mimi swam from left to right and smacked into each other. The crystal drawer in Mimi's arm went flying. Beattie dived for it, her hands shaking. She belly flopped, catching it with her little finger just before it hit the floor. She breathed a sigh of relief.

"Well *done*," Steve whispered as he took a seat on the edge of the drawer, providing *just* enough weight to tip it. The drawer fell from Beattie's finger before she could stop it and landed on the floor with a TING!

"I CAN HEAR YOU!" Hilma roared.

Beattie squeezed her eyes shut.

"Sorrysorrysorrysorrysorry," she heard Steve repeatedly whisper in her ear. She grabbed him and tucked him under her armpit.

He hated that.

"I KNOW YOU'RE IN HERE!" Hilma Snapp shouted. "AND I KNOW YOU STOLE OUR CLAM

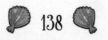

CAR—I SPOTTED IT NEAR THE THEATER, ALL PAINTED AND RUINED!"

"What now?" Zelda whispered.

Beattie held a finger to her lips—she could hear the scratching sound of a tail trailing along the hallway.

Zelda was trying to force a window open, but it wouldn't budge.

"COME OUT RIGHT NOW!" Hilma Snapp screamed. The noise made the sandcastle shake, sending trickles of sand down the walls as the three mermaids floated helplessly on the spot.

Steve squeezed out from under Beattie's armpit, spluttering, as she dared to peer into the hall—she could see Hilma Snapp coming. Her long tail had a curtain of lacelike seaweed covering it, a little like a human wedding dress.

"Hide," Beattie whispered as the twins scattered.

Steve panicked and latched onto Beattie's earlobe.

"OW, STEVE!" she cried.

"Perfect hiding place," he insisted. "She'll just think you have terrible taste in earrings."

Beattie turned to the others. "We'll have to swim over her and out of the fish lips."

Mimi and Zelda looked unsure.

"Ready . . . ," Beattie began, though she wasn't sure if it was a good idea either. "NOW!"

The three of them darted out into the hallway.

"THIEVES!" Hilma Snapp seethed as she watched them soar overhead, hugging the edge of the sandy ceiling.

Zelda and Mimi dived at the fish lips together and disappeared. Beattie closed her eyes and dived after them, but the fish lips barely budged! She clawed her way through with a determined look on her face until there was only her tail to go—and that's when she saw them.

Oysterdale mermaids.

Hundreds of them.

19

Silvia Snapp's Alibi

Beattie tried, without drawing too much attention to herself, to yank her tail from the fish lips. But it was no good, she was stuck. The cluster of Oysterdale mermaids gathered on the lawn stared at her, their embellished tails flicking back and forth in unison.

Hilma glided down from one of the sandcastle's many turrets and swam back and forth in front of the crowd. "I CAUGHT THEM, DIDN'T I!"

"STOP SHOUTING, HILMA!" Silvia Snapp shouted. The two of them turned to face Beattie, identical grins carved on their faces. Silvia Snapp's black hair was pulled into high, taut plaits twisted together and standing perfectly erect on her head. Her nails were as long as the claws of a crocodile but, unlike a crocodile, each was studded with a pearl. She pulled at one of her long nails. By the time she had stopped extending it, and the crowd of Oysterdale mermaids had stopped giggling and squealing, the nail was about as long as Beattie's tail.

"Wh—what are you going to do with that?" Zelda asked, backing up into Beattie's face.

"Get me out," Beattie mumbled into Zelda's tail.

Zelda turned to help her, but Silvia Snapp flicked her

finger, placing the terrifyingly long talon between them and ushering Zelda forward.

"Ah ah ah, no you don't."

The Oysterdale mermaids clapped and started to edge toward them, each pulling at their own talons and lengthening them.

"You didn't think we'd let you leave, after all you've done," Hilma Snapp said with a snigger. "Stealing our car and ruining it, and then breaking into our sandcastle. Tut. Tut. Tut."

Silvia Snapp floated forward. "And how did you get here without the piranhas catching you?"

"What did you do with Arabella Cod?" Beattie demanded.

"Oh, that pufferfish. What do you mean, what did I do with her? She left the Lagoon!" Silvia Snapp cackled, running a finger over her talon to gauge its sharpness.

Beattie got a glimpse of Silvia Snapp's palm. She had the SHOAL stamp! "So you *did* meet with Arabella Cod on the day she went missing," Beattie said. "She was here."

Silvia Snapp wrinkled her nose. "Yes. We had a meeting. But then I called her an old carp, so she left to see Goda Gar in Anchor Rock, who is a slimy little eel."

"And then what?" Beattie pressed as all the other Oysterdale mermaids looked on, confused. "Then what did you do?"

"Why do *you* want to know?" Hilma spat.

Silvia Snapp shot her a look. "Other mermaids are always interested in us, my little fish, because we Oysterdale mermaids are fascinating. And they are boring."

"Yes," Beattie said. "That's the reason why I asked tha—"

"Well, I was in Curly Clips," Silvia Snapp interrupted boastfully. "I went there straight after my meeting for a nice long appointment with Ommy. You know that Ommy, the new Piranha Army chief, lives in the palace. Important. We're friends. He booked the appointment for me and he came too."

"You and Ommy?" Beattie said.

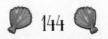

"Yes," Silvia Snapp snapped. "Ommy and me. Hair appointment. Curly Clips."

She pointed a long talon at Beattie's face. "See?" she said to Hilma. "Look how in awe she is."

"No, that's Beattie's OH COD face," Mimi said flatly.

"Now," Silvia Snapp said, weaving her way closer to Zelda, who was edging farther and farther away from the crowd. "We shall have to put you somewhere safe while we alert Ommy. He'll be very interested in you weird little piranha-dodging mermaids." She grabbed Beattie's hand and inspected her nails. "Strange. They have the mark."

20

The Mysterious Mermaid

Far away in the Upper Realms, Belinda Shelton floated by a rock covered in crocodile carvings. She scribbled something in a chunky seaweed notebook.

"YOU'LL BE MY NEXT HAT!" came a shout.

Belinda Shelton looked up, her eyes wide. There, swimming in the near distance, was a mermaid. And she was yelling at a lobster. Something about hats. She wore a veil, her face completely hidden from view, and an armor-like casing of shells over her tail, and she pulled a fat little piranha along on a leash. It looked a little cross-eyed as she dragged it carelessly over rocks.

"HELLO!" Belinda Shelton shouted.

The mermaid turned.

"No," Belinda Shelton gasped, shielding her eyes. "But it's impossible!"

The mermaid was
wearing a shell
top as sunglasses.
They glowed
brightly, the
shells' crocodile
carvings casting
shadows on
the rocks.

Belinda Shelton felt
dizzy just looking at
them. She stumbled back-
ward and grabbed a rock
to steady herself. "The
Ruster Shells," she said
with a squeak. "They're
back."

21

Fish Lips

Beattie was still stuck in the fish lips, and she was beginning to give up. She wasn't a hero; she was just a mermaid. A mermaid stuck in the world's most elaborate sandcastle entrance.

Hilma Snapp's hysterical laughter danced around Smug Street, making the sandcastles shed sprinkles of sand.

Zelda grabbed Beattie's arms and frantically tried to free her.

"Oh dear, no escape!" Silvia Snapp said as the crowd of Oysterdale mermaids cackled.

"LET US GO!" Beattie shouted, pulling wildly at her tail. The fish lips wouldn't budge. Her mind was racing. She needed to distract them so Zelda and Mimi could help pull her free. But what would distract an

Oysterdale mer—"HAVE YOU SEEN MY NEW EARRING?" Beattie roared before she had finished the thought, making the mermaids fall silent.

"Earring?" Silvia Snapp said, clearly intrigued.

"Excuse you, what are you doing?" Steve hissed.

"Go with it," Beattie mumbled out of the side of her mouth. "Wait until we're gone, then do what you do best."

"It's the only talking sea horse earring in the *entire* Lagoon," Beattie said proudly.

"Ooooooh, *accessory*," the Oysterdale mermaids cooed, their talons retracting as they moved closer.

"It's like a pair of earrings . . . but just one," a mermaid said as he reached out to touch it. "I've seen sea horse nose decorations before, but never this . . ."

Hilma Snapp plucked Steve from Beattie's ear and held him up in awe.

"Hello," he said grudgingly.

She jumped and laughed hysterically. "IT REALLY SPEAKS!"

Mimi slowly moved backward. Beattie watched as Zelda nodded at Mimi.

"NOW!" Zelda screamed, diving down toward Beattie as Mimi casually turned and fin-fu chopped the fish lips.

The entire sandcastle crumbled into a pile in one dusty explosion of sand.

"She may talk to sun loungers," Zelda said, "but my twin can topple castles when she wants to."

"MY SANDCASTLE!" Silvia Snapp wailed as Steve slipped from her grasp and fell into the crowd.

"MINE!"

"NO MINE!"

"GIVE THE TALKING EARRING TO ME!"

The mermaids yelled as they tumbled about in a ball, trying desperately to grab Steve. Beattie swam fast with the others down the street. She looked back and saw Hilma angrily trying to squeeze out of the hulking crowd of mermaids all clamoring for the earring.

"THEY'RE GETTING AWAY!" she roared. "THEY'RE GETTING AWAY!"

"We did it!" Zelda said as the three of them dived into the clam car and steered it down a side street and into a cove.

"THE CLAM CAR WAS HERE BUT NOW IT'S GONE!" they heard Hilma Snapp shout. A herd of Oysterdale mermaids tore right past them and straight into the tunnel.

"They think we've gone," Beattie said as she spotted Steve floating outside the window, his eyes narrow.

Beattie opened the clam car so he could swim in. "I'm sorry, Steve. It was the only thing that would distract them!"

Steve swam to his false teeth. "I'LL BE IN MY

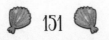

BEDROOM," he said, lifting up the top teeth and swimming in, letting them snap down loudly behind him.

Beattie awkwardly patted the teeth. "Thanks, Steve . . ."

"Let's go to Curly Clips while we're here and they're hunting for us out there," Zelda suggested. "We need to check that Silvia Snapp is telling the truth about her alibi."

22

Curly Clips, the Hairdresser

The clamshell car stuttered its way into the Curly Clips dive-thru and came to an abrupt halt at window one.

"Sabrina Scoosh here, best hairdresser in the Lagoon and winner of the Crab Clipper Style Award. What can I do for you today?"

Her mound of curly hair was decorated with starfish and a coating of sparkly sand.

The three of them just blinked at her.

"Do you have an appointment?" she asked impatiently.

"Nope," Zelda said, sticking her head out of the car window. "But we'd like one."

Before Beattie knew what was happening, the clamshell car roof was whipped back and some incredibly efficient crabs began pruning and plumping their hair.

"I've never seen you around here before," Sabrina said. "Have you always lived in Oysterdale?"

Mimi began to shake her head but Beattie grabbed her plaits. "Maybe you could do something fun with these plaits? And, yes, we've always lived in Oysterdale." She pulled at Mimi's plaits, making her head nod.

"Nothing for me," Zelda said, ducking to avoid the strange assortment of fish that were circling their heads.

"Well, we've got five fishy specials today!" the mermaid said, pointing to a menu on the wall.

"Um," Beattie said, breathing a sigh of relief. The mermaid believed they were from Oysterdale. "I'll have . . . the Cod Curl?"

A substantial cod flopped down and got to work on Beattie.

"Nothing for me," Zelda said again, batting a fish away. "Leave my flick alone."

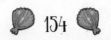

Curly Clips

Dive–Thru Specials

Flat Fish Fluffer—12 clatters
Puffer Fish Flattner—12 clatters
Striped Fish Spritz and Color—25 clatters
Speedy Eel Shock Treatment—19 clatters
Cod Curl—12 clatters

(Please note: Anyone traveling by whale
will not be allowed in the dive–thru
for safety reasons.)

Mimi took a moment to ponder the menu as the cod stretched Beattie's hair beyond recognition, swirling up and letting the hair ping into one single, sculptural, giant, hideous, not-at-all-Beattie curl. "Nothing for me, thanks," Mimi finally said.

"I hate you both," Beattie whispered as a jellyfish hovered in front of her with a mirror.

"And the beauty of it is," Sabrina oozed, "IT'LL LAST FOR DAYS!" She made to snap down the shell roof.

"Wait," Beattie said. "Silvia Snapp told us she was in here the day Arabella Cod was fishnapped."

The mermaid nodded. "Oh yes, she's a regular. Our most famous client. Of course, she comes to me; I *am* the best."

"And did you see Arabella Cod at all that day?" Zelda asked.

"Oh yes, I did. I was outside welcoming Silvia Snapp and Ommy and I saw her at the end of the street. She left through the tunnel. Horrible scowl on her face."

"Really," Beattie mumbled. "So Silvia Snapp was telling the truth."

"Apparently Silvia Snapp called her an old carp," Sabrina said with a shrug.

"So they had their meeting and then Silvia Snapp came here," Beattie pondered. "And how long was Silvia Snapp in here for?" she added as Zelda playfully prodded her new hair.

"Well . . . let's see," the mermaid said, flicking through a book on her counter.

"She had the exclusive Electrifying Eel Plump and Fluff treatment. It takes four hours."

"Four hours," Beattie repeated.

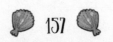

"Four hours," the mermaid said again.

"And Ommy?"

"He had a shorter treatment, a restyle—nice little bob 'do," the hairdresser said. "Just a quick half hour. So lovely of him to book the appointment for her. Mermaids in the other cities say he's evil because of the piranhas, and the fact that he's got them all on lockdown and lets us do whatever we want. But that's only because we're the best, and anyway—would an evil mermaid book the Electrifying Eel Plump and Fluff treatment for a friend? No, I don't think so."

Beattie stared off through the dive-thru hatch, her mind racing. "So Silvia Snapp had her hair done all afternoon." She spotted a poster on the back wall.

"Will that be all?" echoed the distant voice of the Curly Clips mermaid. Beattie's eyes were fixed on the poster.

CURLY CLIPS: THE OFFICIAL HAIRDRESSER
FOR CATWALK SHRIMP!
EVERY DAY AT 6:30.

 158

She remembered what Shelly Shelby had said—she had to bring shells to Silvia Snapp's house on the day Arabella Cod went missing. She was annoyed because Silvia Snapp demanded she go in the evening, when her favorite show was on—*Catwalk Shrimp*.

Beattie turned to the others. "Silvia Snapp was here all afternoon, and with Shelly Shelby in the evening—there's no way she could've fishnapped Arabella Cod."

"Ray Ramona has an alibi for that whole afternoon: he was in Jawella's; so does Liberty Ling: she was playing shockey—the article said so—and Silvia Snapp was at the hairdresser," Mimi said, listing each of the alibis.

"Well then," Zelda said. "It can only be Goda Gar."

23

Um...

Beattie fired up the Clamorado 7 and they took off toward Anchor Rock. It seemed like the only place left that they might find the truth, but Beattie couldn't shake the feeling that they were missing something.

Steve stared at Beattie's new hairdo. "I can fix this, Beattie. I just need a crab, a couple of rocks, and something reeeally stretchy."

"I bet we find our parents in Anchor Rock," Zelda said, nudging Mimi.

"Hopefully not dead," Mimi added.

Zelda flopped in the back seat. "Ugh, why would you say that? You are such a pain in my fin sometimes!" A crab from the hairdresser's, which had stowed away in the back seat, latched a clipper onto her tail. "Ow!" she screamed. "Actual pain in my fin! ACTUAL PAIN IN MY FIN!"

CLAMZINE

GODA GAR

NAME: Goda Gar.

RULER OF: Anchor Rock.

STYLE SIGNIFIER: Her special bird brooch.

FAVORITE PLACE IN ANCHOR ROCK: Her yacht—especially the deck, where she can practice fin-fu.

TOP TIP WHEN VISITING ANCHOR ROCK: Take a trip to the fin-fu master's house, where you can sip warm foam broth and meet the fin-fu master, Mirabel, herself.

MOST LIKELY TO SAY: "And that's the truth."

GODA GAR HAS been chosen to rule over Anchor Rock, the most mysterious of all the Lagoon's regions. A follower of fin-fu, Goda Gar is the SHOAL member we know the least about.

24

To Anchor Rock

The route to Anchor Rock was the most straight-forward of all the journeys you could make in the Lagoon. There was no shell-studded highway, like the one that connected Swirlyshell and Lobstertown, no crystal tunnel or kelp forest, just a stream of clear water through a deep and deserted canyon. Yet very few mermaids from Swirlyshell or anywhere else in the Lagoon made the trip to Anchor Rock. It was colder up there, with straight-talking mermaids and myths that those who knew them only dared to whisper. Like the one about the mermaid who cursed you if you whispered.

To Beattie's left, she could just make out the rugged caves and in the distance the ghostly bow of the *Merry Mary*. Jellyfish bobbed in large clumps outside it. Not a single mermaid had ever ventured inside. Beattie's mom had gotten close once, but then she'd met Steve and gotten distracted.

Beattie pulled the lever above her head and the clam car shot forward and through the city's stylish gates, past the ANCHOR ROCK sign, which was crowned with the original anchor the city was named after. The anchor had once belonged to the *Merry Mary*, or so Beattie had heard. Beyond the sign sat a gigantic steel structure known as Anchor Avenue, with treelike coral lining the sides. Off the avenue were old shipping containers and small sunken ships, dragged to the depths by mermaids who had dared to travel to the Upper Realms.

A smartly dressed mermaid with a shimmering tail floated past on an old, bent bicycle pulled by an eel in a shell tank top. He ducked between two ancient wooden boats when he saw a clump of piranhas swimming past.

"That's it, I think," Beattie said, pointing at a large yacht in the distance. "And that must be her."

A mermaid with perfect silver hair tied in a plait above her head was floating on the starboard side looking stern.

Zelda pulled out the *Clamzine* she'd taken from Silvia Snapp's sandcastle. "That's her all right. And *look*," she said, tapping the tiny brooch Goda Gar was wearing in the picture. "A *swan*."

Mimi and Beattie looked at each other.

"A swan!" Zelda cried. "That proves it!"

"Zelda," Beattie said slowly, inspecting the magazine. "That's an ostrich."

"Oh, right," Zelda said, taking a closer look. "Are they different?"

Steve opened the false teeth and poked his head out. "I can't believe you're reading that *Clamzine* when a brand-new issue has been stuck to the back window for hours."

"What?!" Beattie cried as she shot out of the car and grabbed it.

CLAMZINE

BELINDA SHELTON SEARCHES FOR THE CROCODILE KINGDOM IN UPPER REALM 5 AND MAKES HER MOST INCREDIBLE DISCOVERY YET

Deep in the waters of Upper Realm 5, there are all sorts of new wonders to discover. And there is Swamp Eye, a rare and itchy eye infection, which I currently have.

The water is murky here and the crocodiles are friendly enough. I discovered a strange shell-studded arch deep in one of the canyons, but I couldn't reach it; the crocodiles surrounded me and forced me back up to the surface. It is the most convincing evidence I've come across that the hidden mermaid Crocodile Kingdom really exists.

I also tried shouting, "HELLO, LET ME IN PLEASE." But no luck.

That's when I heard a voice. I turned to see a mermaid wearing a lace veil, her tail covered in shells. But the most astonishing thing was the traditional shell top she was wearing on her face, as if it was a pair of sunglasses.

SHE WAS WEARING THE RUSTER SHELLS.

It was the original top! I could tell because the shells nearly blinded me.

She disappeared before I could speak to her or find out who she was. I am convinced she was a Crocodile Kingdom mermaid. It can't be Mary Ruster, because she's dead.

TOP TIP WHEN TRAVELING TO THE AREA:
Leave your eyes at home, unless you want to get Swamp Eye.
NEXT STOP: Viperview Prison, Upper Realm 1

Beattie stared blankly at the article. "My mom saw a mermaid from the Crocodile Kingdom wearing the Ruster Shells."

"Oh yes, the shells Mary Ruster wore that put everyone in a trance in the Year of the Pufferfish," Mimi said airily.

"Pardon, what?" Beattie said. "A trance?"

"The Ruster Shells are magic," Mimi said.

"Magic?" Zelda said. "What are we—witches?"

"No, they look different," Steve said.

"Everyone who does fin-fu knows the legend of the Ruster Shells," Mimi said. "Mary Ruster, the mermaid who owned the Ruster Shells, was really good at fin-fu. I mentioned it not so long ago when we were on the Crabbyshell Highway, when you read the article about mermaid tops, Beattie. Then Zelda shouted something and grabbed my binoculars."

"Wait, explain to me exactly what the legend of the Ruster Shells is," Beattie said.

"Mary Ruster was one clumsy mermaid," Mimi began. "She was always breaking and sinking things, like the time she sank the *Merry Mary* by accident. It was that very day that she found two magic shells with crocodiles carved on them. They were wedged in one of the masts."

"I've never heard so much nonsense in all my life!" Zelda said with a snort.

Mimi stuck her nose in the air and continued. "My fin-fu master, Mirabel, says that according to the legend, Mary Ruster didn't know the shells were magic. She just thought they would make an excellent shell top, and she was having a summer ball in the palace that they would be just perfect for. On the night of the ball, she glided into the room wearing the shells and—"

Steve gasped. "Oh, sorry," he said. "Too early. Keep going."

Mimi lowered her voice to a whisper. "And all the mermaids fell into a trance."

"A *trance*?" Zelda said mockingly.

"It took her years to figure out why all the mermaids were being so weird and doing everything she said," Mimi continued, with a casual shrug. "So to protect the Lagoon from the strange shells, which became known as the Ruster Shells, she hid them somewhere secret and safe, and they haven't been seen since."

"So she just pointed these 'magic' shells at the mermaids and it put them in a trance?" Zelda asked.

 168

Mimi cracked her knuckles and did a little fin-fu chop with her finger. "Most mermaids who know the story of the Ruster Shells believe it had something to do with the shell tops they all wore back then. Mermaids were made to wear the same thing in those days. It's not like today, when we can wear whatever we think is nice—shoulder pads, Clippee tees, small shells, big shells. Apparently, there was only one mermaid at the ball who wasn't put in a trance and that was actress Maisie Swimple, who was wearing forty-nine glittered shrimp as part of a costume for the entertainment section of the ball."

Some fish swam in and out of Beattie's gaping mouth.

"Well, there you go," Zelda said. "Proof that you should always be free to wear whatever you want, even if what you want to wear is glittered shrimp."

"And Mary Ruster had a pet dolphin called Mr. Bottle," Mimi added, "which is a fact about her that I've always liked."

Beattie looked from the article to Mimi and back again. "That's it, Mimi! THAT'S WHY EVERYONE

HAS TO MAKE THOSE SHELL TOPS FOR THE SWAN! They're going to put every single mermaid in a trance."

"Oh come on, Beattie," Zelda said. "The Ruster Shells? It's just a story. It's as real as Clippee the cartoon lobster in a dress."

"CLIPPEE IS REAL, YOU MONSTER!" Steve screamed.

"What if it's not a silly story," Beattie said urgently. "What if The Swan is trying to recreate what happened all those years ago. What if the Ruster Shells are really back?"

They turned to look at Goda Gar in the distance.

"If you're right," Zelda said slowly, "then that mermaid over there has managed to fishnap Arabella Cod and find the most dangerous and well-hidden shells in Lagoon history . . . And we're about to go and spy on her with nothing but Mimi's cobbled-together binoculars and a yappy sea horse."

25

Goda Gar's Yacht House

The four of them swam fast, winding in and out of the boats and shipping containers. When they got to Goda Gar's grand yacht they pasted themselves flat against the side of it.

"We need to find a way in," Beattie whispered.

Zelda tried to open one of the large porthole windows. It didn't budge. She hit it.

An alarm sounded. Beattie glared at her.

"What?" Zelda huffed. "Who puts an alarm on a sunken yacht?"

"You there!" Goda Gar cried. "What are you doing?"

Mimi pointed at the window and was about to explain they were trying to spy, but Beattie pushed her out of the way before she could say anything, frantically lunged forward, plucked Steve from where he was floating and

yelled, "WE'RE SELLING TALKING SEA HORSES." She held him up.

"Talking sea horses?" Goda Gar said, an eyebrow raised. "How much?"

"Only fifty clatters!" Beattie cheered.

"*FIFTY CLATTERS?*" Steve scoffed.

"One hundred clatters!" Beattie said, looking at Steve for approval. Steve shook his head.

"Seriously?" Beattie whispered. "A hundred clatters is a lot."

"For a—*miracle*?" Steve asked grandly.

"It's just so she lets us in, Steve," Beattie hissed. "It's not really what I think you're worth. I'm not going to say a ridiculous number like—"

"*ONE TRILLION CLATTERS!*" Steve said, doing his best Beattie impression.

Zelda shook her head. "Can't believe you still have that thing."

Mimi looked at him. "I didn't realize you were so expensive. I think it's because you sleep in false teeth."

"IT'S A BEDROOM!" Steve roared.

Goda Gar floated through the dark glass cabin and opened a door for them on the back deck. "Come on in," she said with a grimace.

Goda Gar's yacht was very chic. It had long benches with simple seaweed cushions, a huge bar shaped like an oyster shell, and a viewing deck that looked out across Anchor Rock, all the way south to the spires of Swirlyshell.

"I'll get us some Kelpskey," Goda Gar said, before quickly disappearing into another room.

The three of them, and Steve, sat in silence.

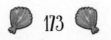

"I'm scared," Zelda eventually whispered to Mimi. "What if she's going to get a weapon?"

"She said she was going to get Kelpskey," Mimi replied casually, staring blankly ahead.

"She could be making it up!" Zelda said. "She could be perfecting a recipe to make the three of us into fish soup. With sea horse croutons!"

"Shhh," Beattie pleaded. "She might hear you."

"Hear you?" Goda Gar said as she appeared behind them, making the four of them SCREAM. She plunked down a tray of Kelpskey drinks, which made them SCREAM again.

"I get the impression you're scared of me," she said.

"Zelda is," Mimi said.

"I'm not!" Zelda protested.

"We're not scared," Beattie said. "We're simple talking-sea-horse salesmen." She shook her head when she realized how stupid it sounded.

"And you're from around here, are you?" Goda Gar said, pointing at their tails. Most of the mermaids in Anchor Rock had gray tails with a sparkly edge.

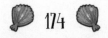

174

"We moved here a long time ago, from Swirlyshell," Beattie lied. "And set up our talking-sea-horse business. It's *booming.*"

"Is that so," Goda Gar said, staring at Beattie. She had an intimidating stare—like her pale gray eyes could see right through you.

Beattie cleared her throat. "Were you planning to meet with Arabella Cod on the day she went missing, but she didn't show up?"

"It's a question we always ask," Zelda added quickly, "when selling talking sea horses . . ."

"Are you trying to figure out what happened to Arabella Cod?" Goda Gar asked.

They all held their breath.

This is it, Beattie thought. *We're dead fish.*

Goda Gar wriggled in between them. "Because *I've* been trying to figure it out too."

Beattie noticed Goda Gar didn't have the SHOAL stamp on her hand.

"What happened that day?" Beattie asked.

"Well," Goda Gar began, "I said I'd meet Arabella Cod

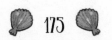

at Eely Good Fashions. I had to be there all afternoon anyway, to sign eel tank tops, you see. I waited for hours. When she didn't arrive, I swam to the palace to see what was going on. I was a little angry she'd forgotten about me. Mermaids in Swirlyshell are always forgetting about us up here in the north. But when I arrived at the palace everyone was gone, so I turned and went straight back. I spotted Liberty Ling on the way home, with a large whale. I told her everyone was missing from the palace, and about Arabella Cod. I told her to watch out."

"In the afternoon?" Beattie asked. "With a whale?"

"Yes, a whale, in the afternoon," Goda Gar said with a nod. "She's from Lobstertown, after all. It was probably art or something."

"I bet you can't prove you were at Eely Good Fashions," Zelda said, gripping one of the seaweed cushions in fear. "It doesn't even sound like a real place."

"Do you have proof that you were at Eely Good Fashions?" Beattie asked, unsure what Goda Gar might do when they uncovered the truth—would she attack?

"It's a new shop, Eely Good Fashions," Goda Gar said.

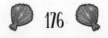

"It sells tank tops and accessories for pet eels. They covered it in our local newspaper, *Ahoy*." She handed Beattie a report about the opening. It had a picture of her there and everything. "And there are about one hundred mermaids who can confirm I was there all afternoon."

It was a solid alibi.

"Well . . . then no one did it," Zelda said, slumping. "Ray Ramona, Liberty Ling, Silvia Snapp, and now you. You all have alibis."

Beattie twisted her fingers through her plait. The yacht seemed like it was spinning. "It's so simple!" she cried, twirling on her tail.

"What is it, Beattie?" Steve asked, swimming around her. "*Calm down.*"

She grabbed the side of the yacht and looked out to the Lagoon stretching off into the distance. "I know who it was!" she announced. "I KNOW WHO DID IT!"

"Who?!" they all said at once.

Beattie turned to them and grinned. "There's only one mermaid on that list who was in two places at once that day . . . and *no* mermaid can be in two places at once."

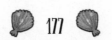 177

CLAMZINE

LIBERTY LING

LIBERTY LING HAS been chosen to rule over Lobstertown, the Lagoon's most loved city—home of artists Ruby Scales and Alfonso Munch, and the birthplace of some of the Lagoon's most talented young sports stars, including shockey stars Rachel Rocker and Liberty Ling herself. Liberty Ling is also a scholar and expert in mermaid history, most notably the Ruster dynasty, and has big plans for the city. Here's what you need to know about her.

NAME: Liberty Ling.

RULER OF: Lobstertown.

STYLE SIGNIFIER: Her long bangs and shell-studded designer glasses by Crabby Crabby Four Eyes.

FAVORITE PLACE IN LOBSTERTOWN: The Clipper Library, where she reads about the Lagoon's history. She spent many days studying the Science of Shells when she was a student at Claw University.

TOP TIP WHEN VISITING LOBSTERTOWN: Take a tour of the new funfair next door to the Orange Bucket. You can do everything from riding the Whale Splash, a brand-new attraction, to painting—at the moment they are asking young mermaids to help us paint fun things on the outside of the Orange Bucket café.

MOST LIKELY TO SAY: "SHOCKEY! SHOCKEY! SHOCKEY!"

26

Brilliant Beattie

"The Swan...is LIBERTY LING," Beattie said triumphantly as the three of them, and Steve, huddled together sipping Kelpskey. It was getting dark, and Goda Gar's eel was busy preparing a platter of fancy sponge bites and shells filled with sweet whipped foam. Beattie tucked her tail under her. It was cold in Anchor Rock, even in the yacht.

Goda Gar shook her head in disbelief.

"You saw Liberty Ling with a whale that afternoon," Beattie explained. "But according to the article in *Clamzine* that Ray Ramona gave us, at that time she was also playing in a shockey match in Lobstertown."

"So...how did she do it?" Zelda asked. "A whole arena of mermaids would notice if she was gone, and

Goda Gar couldn't have seen her with a whale if she wasn't there."

"It took me a while to figure it out." Beattie grinned. "It's all about what happened at Curly Clips."

"Curly Clips?" Mimi said. "But that was Silvia Snapp's alibi."

Beattie shook her head. "But what hairstyle did the Curly Clips mermaid say *Ommy* got? A short bob 'do." She held up the *Clamzine*, pointing at the pictures of the SHOAL. "The same hairstyle as Liberty Ling."

"So . . . wait? You think Ommy disguised himself as Liberty Ling?"

Beattie nodded.

"So which one was Ommy? The one who hundreds of mermaids saw at the shockey match, or the one Goda Gar saw?"

"I've been thinking about that," Beattie said, curling the corner of the *Clamzine* in her fingers. "I don't think Goda Gar would be fooled, but a whole arena of mermaids might be, looking at Liberty Ling from afar. I think they switched halfway through the match—I

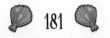 181

think all the action happened during halftime at the shockey match—at 3 p.m."

"Go on," Steve said eagerly.

"Think about it," Beattie said. "Silvia Snapp offends Arabella Cod, calls her an old carp. Arabella Cod leaves Oysterdale and heads to Anchor Rock to meet Goda Gar. It's about an hour away, all the way in the north. Meanwhile, Ommy is getting his hair done and Liberty Ling is playing in a shockey match. At 3 p.m., the first half of the shockey match finishes. By that point, Arabella Cod would be halfway to Anchor Rock—and where would she be close to at that point?"

Mimi drew a map of the Lagoon on the carpet with squid ink.

"Careful with the carpe—oh, never mind," Goda Gar said.

"Lobstertown," Mimi said. "She'd be near Lobstertown."

"Exactly," Beattie said. "Liberty Ling sneaks away from the stadium at halftime, changes out of her shockey gear, and races out of Lobstertown and catches

182

Arabella Cod on the outskirts on her way to Anchor Rock. And she fishnaps her."

"Where does she put her?" Steve asked, leaping about excitedly.

Beattie paused. "That I haven't figured out yet. So, Liberty Ling is fishnapping Arabella Cod, *meanwhile*,

Ommy finishes his quick hair appointment—his hair now looks like Liberty Ling's—and swims fast to Lobstertown. Again, that would take about half an hour, just in time for the second half of the shockey match. He sneaks into the stadium, puts on Liberty Ling's shockey gear, and poses as her for the rest of the tournament. Look at the difference in the goals Liberty Ling scored in the first half and the second," Beattie said, brandishing the *Clamzine*. "One hundred and four points in the first half and only two points in the second. It's like two different mermaids were playing—because two different mermaids *were* playing."

"So, what happened to all the palace mermaids?" Zelda asked. "If you're right, that explains when Arabella Cod was fishnapped, but what about the others?"

Beattie grinned again and raised a finger. "They were probably . . . in the whale!"

"WHAT?!" Zelda shouted.

"So, not piranha food?" Mimi asked.

"A whale. A WHALE," Zelda said again. "Our parents were in a massive WHALE?!"

Beattie bit her lip and nodded. She had completely forgotten that Zelda and Mimi's parents worked at the palace. "Liberty Ling would have plenty of time to hide Arabella Cod, go to the palace with a whale, convince everyone to get in, and then take them and hide them too—all by the time Goda Gar got to the palace at 6 p.m. When Goda Gar passed Liberty Ling and the whale, Liberty Ling had probably just come from the palace. The mermaids from the palace were in the whale!"

"It was swimming a bit funnily...," Goda Gar recalled.

"But a whale would spit them out after a couple of hours," Mimi pointed out. "Whales have rules about that sort of thing."

"True," Beattie mused. "Which means the whale was just a temporary place to stash the mermaids—a way to transport them to somewhere more permanent. But *where*, that's the question..."

27

Ommy Flips

Ommy floated across the Periwinkle Palace kitchen and placed a bejewelled bowl in front of Nom.

"There you go, my little Nom Nom."

Nom sank his teeth into Ommy's tail. There was nothing he hated more than being called *Nom Nom*.

The small shell on the countertop started jiggling. Ommy flipped it open and began shouting.

"HAVE YOU SEEN THE BELINDA SHELTON ARTICLE IN *CLAMZINE*?! SHE SAW YOU! SHE SAW THE RUSTER SHELLS!"

"Impossible," The Swan said. "I swam past her really fast."

Ommy couldn't see a clear picture of The Swan in the shell; all he could see was the two gigantic shining Ruster Shells, which she was still wearing like sunglasses.

"I can't wait to wear the Ruster Shells and my new crocodile-shaped hat to the shockey," she oozed.

"We can't afford for the mermaids to figure out what we're up to before it's done, especially the clever SHOAL mermaids," Ommy ranted. "They've been meddling too much as it is."

One of Ray Ramona's spy sharks floated slowly past the window. It had SPY SHARK 1108 painted on its side.

"What are you up to?" The Swan asked, sounding confused.

Ommy scrunched up his fists. "We're going to have to tweak the plan!" He whistled, and watched as a long line of piranhas snaked into the room . . .

28

A Fishnap

Beattie could hear the calming sound of water trickling through Goda Gar's grand old yacht. It was all lit up now, with strings of bulbs hanging from mast to mast. Now that Beattie knew who The Swan really was, stopping her suddenly seemed achievable. She winced at the thought of all the clues they'd missed. She poured some more Kelpskey and shoved a delicious sea sponge in her mouth. "Zelda, do you remember Old Wonky said your parents left the palace willingly? That would make sense—Liberty Ling probably arrived at the palace with some lie that Arabella Cod had ordered them to board the whale. They would trust a SHOAL member."

"A WHALE?" Zelda said again. "I bet they went all wrinkly in there . . ."

"*And,*" Beattie went on, "do you remember Old Wonky kept jumping on the Lobstertown throne! He was trying to tell us it was Liberty Ling of Lobstertown all along!"

Mimi scooped some sweet foam from a shell, tipping it into her mouth to get the last drops.

"You should stay here tonight," Goda Gar said as she soared into the room with another tray of treats. "I got the eels to put your clam car on the bow of the boat, for safekeeping."

Beattie stretched out on the floor and studied the *Clamzine* profile of Liberty Ling. She never wanted to leave Goda Gar's cozy yacht. "You know," she said, through a mouthful of sea sponge, "Liberty Ling studied the Science of Shells. She must've figured out where the Ruster Shells were. That's pretty impressive—the first mermaid to do so in hundreds of years."

"Great," Zelda said, flopping onto a bench and sending the seaweed cushions flying. "We have a *clever* nemesis."

Mimi clinked her glass against Beattie's and flopped down next to her on the floor. "We'll defeat her."

"When do you think she's going to strike?" Zelda

asked. "You know, with the whole putting-everyone-in-a-trance thing?"

"I don't know," Beattie said. "But we need to look out for anything to do with Liberty Ling and the shell tops. And it would need to be big."

Goda Gar flapped her tail frantically and glided across the room. She returned with a flyer. "Like *this*? The piranhas and Oysterdale mermaids were handing them out just a couple of hours ago."

Beattie snatched it from her and frowned.

Liberty Ling announces biggest Lobstertown
shockey tournament ever.
The game will see all five regions
competing tomorrow.
The Swan demands all mermaids in the Lagoon attend.
Shell tops must be worn, or you will be eaten
by the piranhas.

"What's the Lobsterdome slogan again, Zelda?" Beattie asked, not taking her eyes off the flyer.

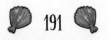

"*A seat for every mermaid!*" Zelda said.

"This is it," Beattie said with a gulp. "She has the Ruster Shells and she's going to use them—on every mermaid in one fell swoop!"

"I can alert Ray Ramona," Goda Gar said. "I'll tell him to bring sharks to the stadium. If we start now, we can alert a lot of mermaids."

"But there are millions all over the Lagoo—"

BANG!

Beattie leaped up.

The yacht alarm sounded. The lights began to flash.

"Quick," Goda Gar said, ushering them from the lounge and onto the bow of the boat. "Get in the clam car."

Beattie caught a glimpse of what was waiting at the side of the yacht. Half the Piranha Army, jaws gnashing.

"What's going on?" Zelda whispered as the three of them squeezed into the car. There was nothing but silence, then a rumbling noise. The yacht seemed to shake.

Steve emerged from his false teeth, yawning, his shell top askew.

Beattie nervously pressed a couple of buttons on the

 192

dashboard and the clam car slowly swiveled so the windshield was facing the right way.

She whimpered and covered her mouth. Zelda shielded Mimi's eyes. Steve darted into his false teeth, squealing, "FISHNAP!"

There, on the bow, was Goda Gar, being tied up with seaweed streams and carted off by the chomping piranhas.

"Why are they taking her?" Beattie said, placing a hand on the windshield. "We have to stop them." She made to open the clam car roof, but Zelda stopped her.

"Don't, Beattie, there's nothing we can do. We have to stop Liberty Ling. The only thing working in our favor is that she doesn't seem to know we exist. But she will if you try to stop those piranhas."

Beattie turned and her heart lurched so far and so fast it felt like it had high-fived her brain. A sinister figure with a bob hairdo was snaking across the bow of the boat and heading straight for the clam car.

"Ommy," Beattie whispered as the three of them cowered in their seats.

He wove closer and closer, his eyes narrowing as he approached the little car nestled below the yacht's flashing lights.

There was another *BANG*! Then a strange squeak.

Beattie peeked out just in time to see Ommy spin around and peer over the edge of the yacht.

"OH NOT AGAIN, NOM! STOP TRYING TO STEAL THAT EEL'S TANK TOP!"

Ommy dived over the side of the yacht and disappeared.

The three of them exhaled loudly and sat in startled silence, staring blankly ahead.

Steve peeked out of his false teeth. "Well, I think we can all agree, eel tank tops are *excellent*."

"Now what?" Zelda said, slumping back in her seat. "Should we drive around, shouting about Liberty Ling and her plan? Mimi could refashion her shell binoculars as a *megaphone*."

Beattie thought for a moment. "What if they don't believe us? Plus, we don't have enough time to alert everyone. One of the Oysterdale mermaids could catch us. No . . . it's too risky. We need to surprise Liberty Ling at the match. She and Ommy must not suspect a thing, until it's too late."

Mimi and Zelda exchanged glances.

"So," Zelda said eventually, "what's the plan?"

Beattie pulled out the flyer.

"Liberty Ling is playing in the match," Zelda said, craning her neck so she could read it.

"You should dress up in your shockey gear and mark her," Beattie said. "Take the place of another mermaid on the Swirlyshell team. I'm sure Rachel Rocker or Riley Ramona could sneak you into the locker rooms. And then you could alert the other players."

Zelda nodded.

"And if she's wearing the Ruster Shells—crush them," Beattie added, scrunching up her fist.

"If she's wearing them, they'll be hidden under her shockey pads," Mimi pointed out. "Because they glow *really* brightly."

"Could you get close enough to potentially crush them?" Beattie asked.

Zelda nodded. "I can probably make her collide with one of the Swirlyshell team's dolphins, or have a shark chomp at her, or something."

"Good," Beattie said. "Get all the players involved, apart from the Oysterdale Wonders, of course. I'll try to find Ray Ramona and tell him what's going on. He can help us deal with Ommy."

Steve floated above his false teeth.

"Steve, you will try to find one of those tannoy things and make an announcement that Liberty Ling is The Swan."

"Can I do it in a funny accent?" he asked.

Beattie nodded. "As long as it's in Mermaid and not some strange sea horse language."

"Hopple bun top zet!" Steve said angrily.

Beattie wiggled further down in her seat as Zelda pulled the shell curtain. "I suppose we'd better sleep in here tonight, Beatts," she said. "In case we need to make a quick getaway."

Beattie nodded. She could feel her eyes closing. It had been a long day. The clam car was so cozy, all their tails tangled together.

Zelda snuggled into Mimi, ready to doze off.

"Wait," Mimi said. "What part am I going to play in the plan?"

Beattie closed her eyes and grinned. "You, Mimi, get the best part."

29

Lobstertown

Lobstertown glowed brightly in hues of red and purple, its buildings sculptural masterpieces designed by famous mermaid architects. It was all bright lights and flashing images of Clippee the cartoon lobster in a dress. Lobstertown was the art city, the one with the buzz, the one all young mermaids wanted to move to as soon as they left school.

Beattie and Zelda knew Lobstertown well, unlike the other places in the Lagoon. It was a Swirlyshell mermaid thing to take the whale bus to Lobstertown on weekends and have foam shakes at the Orange Bucket café. It loomed large in the distance—a giant replica of a bucket, painted orange and decorated with a slide that looped around and around, all the way from top to bottom.

They passed a building with a huge moving billboard showing Clippee dancing next to Nose, his sea horse sidekick.

Clippee, Clippee, Clippee, Clippee, Clippee WHOA!
Clippee, Clippee, Clippee, Clippee, Clippee OH!
Clippee, Clippee, Clippee, Clippee, Clippee WHOA!
Clippee, Clippee, Clippee, Clippee, Clippee,
Clippee, Clippee, Clippee, Clippee, Clippee,
Clippee, Clippee—SHOW!

"*It's the Clippee show!*" went the jingle blaring from the screen. Beattie looked back to see Steve bobbing up and down to the music. Zelda was rolling her eyes.

Beattie steered the clam car along the road, coming to a halt at the traffic light, which was just two lobsters mounted on a beautiful stone pillar. They took turns scuttling up to the top with either a STOP or a SWIM sign. In the background she could see a neon billboard showing a huge cartoon of Clippee's archnemesis, O, the pufferfish, in a curly wig.

"He's my favorite cartoon character," Zelda said, deliberately winding Steve up. "Evil O."

Steve gasped. "Excuse you! He's THE WORST!"

"I hope Mimi is getting on okay," Beattie mumbled. "If her part of the plan fails . . ."

"She's *fine*, she's probably done it already," Zelda said confidently. "Or she's chatting to a tuna. It is *Mimi*, after all."

Up ahead, thousands of mermaids were filing into the Lobsterdome wearing shell tops and their shockey fan gear—everything from red-and-purple-spotted gloves and caps to chunky silver headbands covered in toy sharks. But unlike at normal shockey matches, the mermaids were all wearing traditional shell tops—some were actually wearing them as tops, others as sunglasses, some as earmuffs, and one mermaid was wearing them as some rather fabulous shoulder pads. Piranhas swarmed around the mermaids, making them wince.

Beattie turned to Zelda, who was eagerly pulling on her shell-studded gloves, followed by the shell elbow pads. She pulled large shell shoulder pads from her bag

and put them on, followed by, finally, a shell-studded helmet.

"That's Zelda Swish over there, I think," came a whisper from the crowd as Zelda rolled out of the car. She was quite a famous shockey player in the Lagoon. Zelda raised an arm, ready to wave, when Rachel Rocker dived at her.

"Oh, Zelda!" she cried. "I've been looking for you and Mimi and Beattie. Where is Mimi?"

"Fishing," Zelda said with a smirk.

"Shelly Shelby saw The Swan!" Rachel Rocker cried. "She said to tell you she wears a lace veil and shells all over her tail. Still doesn't know who it is, though. But that's something, isn't it?"

"We know who it is," Beattie said, distracted by the crowd. "It's Liberty Ling."

"Really?" Rachel Rocker said, clearly taken aback. "Well, that would explain the shells on the tail. She's hiding a lobster tail!"

Zelda tapped her helmet.

"Wait," Rachel Rocker said. "Are you playing?"

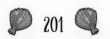

"I am now," Zelda said with a wink. "Can you get me into the shockey locker rooms?"

"Meet me at the locker-room door in five minutes," Rachel Rocker said, giving her a nod.

Beattie slammed the lid down on the clam car as she watched Rachel Rocker slip inside the stadium. Groups of mermaids pointed at Rachel and screamed with delight.

"SHE'S THE BEST!" a mermaid oozed, wearing an "I ♥ RACHEL ROCKER" T-shirt.

"Ready?" Beattie said breathlessly.

Zelda tapped her helmet. "Obviously."

"Not really, if I'm honest," Steve said.

"The most important thing," Beattie said, "is that we destroy those shells."

203

CLAMZINE

SHOCKEY 101—A MERMAID'S GUIDE TO THE GAME

Despite being the number-one mermaid sport, a little over a third of the Lagoon—that's nearly 500,000 mermaids—have never seen a shockey match. As we're all being forced to attend one by order of Piranha Army Chief Ommy and the mysterious Swan, here's what you need to know if you're a mermaid who doesn't know the game, as told by Swirlyshell's star swimmer, Rachel Rocker!

There are five shockey teams—one for each of the Lagoon's towns and cities. There are the Oysterdale Wonders, who always cheat, and the Swirlyshell Shots, who are completely the best. Then you've got the Anchor Rockers, the Hammerhead Heavyweights, and the Lobstertown Loons. Us Swirlyshell Shots are pretty good friends with the Lobstertown Loons, so we don't mind that they're winning almost every match at the moment.

Each team has eight players. Six of the players on the team are riders. The other two are swimmers, like me. The track is a giant circle, and the swimmers score points by swimming around the circle and passing the checkpoint with the shockey pawn.

The shockey pawn is a human shoe. No one knows why, but it is.

But it's not so easy to swim all the way around the track, because the riders from the other team try to stop you, while the riders on your team try to stop the swimmers on the other team. Got it?

The riders on the different teams ride the course on different creatures. The Oysterdale Wonders ride decorated octopuses with lethal diamond-studded tentacles. The Lobstertown Loons ride lobster carts, which are flimsy but fast. The Hammerhead Heavyweights are on saddled sharks, and the Anchor Rockers balance on razorfish—some say they look like humans on things called skis, but I don't know what they are. And we Swirlyshell Shots? We ride decked-out dolphins.

Enjoy the game!

30

The Lobsterdome

Beattie swam fast into the Lobsterdome. The thundering sound of thousands of mermaids was deafening. She fiddled with the shell top she'd tied to her plait. Zelda had decided to strap hers to her wrist. They didn't want to not wear them and make any of the piranhas or Oysterdale mermaids suspicious but, equally, the thought of forgetting it was tied in her hair and being put in a trance was making Beattie nervous.

"STEVE!" she shouted over the roar of the crowd. "FIND SOMEWHERE TO MAKE THE ANNOUNCEMENT! THE PLAN, STEVE!"

Steve bowed and floated off. Beattie watched him head straight, before veering wildly to the left when he spotted a moving billboard showing Clippee dancing.

"Oh cods," Beattie said under her breath.

He pasted himself
against the screen
and started
jiggling,
pretending
he was
Nose, the
cartoon
sea horse.

"MOVE
OUT OF
THE WAY!" a
mermaid shouted.

"THAT SEA HORSE IS RUINING THE CLIPPEE CARTOON!" shouted another.

"I'm replacing Nose as Clippee's new sidekick!" Steve yelled proudly.

"YOU'RE NOT EVEN A CARTOON!"

Beattie rolled her eyes as she wriggled her way through a group of mermaids and up to the rail that separated the shouting crowds from the players.

Up high, in the royal box, she could see a cluster of mermaids and an octopus waiter. She craned her neck, pushing a couple of mermaids in front of her out of the way. There was a clump of piranhas up there too.

"Ray Ramona's got to be there," she said as she fought her way through the crowds. She passed a loud group of Hammerhead Heights mermaid fans, decked out in silver Hammerhead Heavyweights T-shirts under their handmade shell tops.

One of them turned to her. "Do you know if Riley Ramona is playing? He's my *favorite*."

Beattie shrugged and kept on swimming. There was a BANG! She dived to the ground, looking up nervously just in time to see that it was only a bunch of elaborately adorned sea creatures bursting from the changing rooms. They swam into the arena and began doing warm-up laps—octopuses wearing flamboyant hats, dolphins clad in shell-studded saddles, a cart constructed entirely of linked-up lobsters, sharks with squid-ink masks, and razorfish, which the Anchor Rock mermaids were strapping to the tips of their tails.

Beattie swam fast around the edge of the arena as the teams of mermaids from each of the five cities mounted the octopuses, leaped into the dolphins' saddles, slipped into lobster carts, and sat neatly atop the sharks. The Anchor Rock mermaids zipped about with the razorfish attached to their tails, moving faster than all the others. She spotted Zelda and Rachel Rocker wrapping seaweed ribbons around a dolphin and whispering to each other.

Beattie stopped as Liberty Ling glided into the arena to wild applause. There was no glow, no evidence she was wearing the Ruster Shells. But she was clad head-to-toe in shell armor. Zelda looked up and spotted Beattie in the crowd. She gave her a thumbs-up and pulled her heavy helmet on.

"THREE! TWO! ONE! ... SHOCKEY!" a voice roared from the tannoy. Beattie looked around, hoping to see Steve doing something useful. But he was still dancing next to the Clippee cartoon.

The match began. Zelda raced after Liberty Ling, and tried to dart through a gap between two octopuses but was batted to the side.

Beattie winced and covered her eyes.

"GO, SLAMMIT JANET!" the crowd on the Swirlyshell side screamed.

Mermaids and sea creatures careered around the track and past a large octopus holding paddles with each of their emblems.

"POINT TO LOBSTERTOWN!" came a roar as Beattie saw Zelda shake her head.

Beattie watched as one of the Oysterdale mermaids spun her octopus aggressively and took out one of the Hammerhead Heavyweights with its chunky, sucker-covered arms.

"BAD FISH! BAD FISH!" a mermaid shouted (the underwater term for FOUL!).

"GET USED TO IT!" an Oysterdale mermaid squealed from the other side of the track.

Beattie swam faster through the crowds, pushing mermaids to the side. She was almost at the royal box. She spotted Ray Ramona! His back was turned.

"RAY RAMONA!" she shouted, the whole arena nothing but a blur of shark teeth, tumbling mermaids, and bobbing dolphins. The crowd groaned in unison. Beattie turned to the track just in time to see Zelda go flying, all the way past two Lobstertown mermaids, between a Hammerhead shark and past an Anchor Rock mermaid riding two razorfish to—

BAM!

"POINT FOR SWIRLYSHELL!"

Zelda turned and gave the crowd a thumbs-up.

Beattie rolled her eyes. Zelda was *supposed* to be marking Liberty Ling! She turned back to Ray Ramona.

"RAY RAMONA!" Beattie tried again. "I NEED TO—"

Slowly he turned, and that's when she saw them. Angry piranhas were pulling a tight seaweed binding around Ray Ramona's hands. There was a chomp chop stuffed in his mouth! And not in a good way.

"Mueetie," he mumbled, just as a cold hand grabbed Beattie's arm.

"And where do you think *you're* going, Beattie Shelton?"

Beattie turned around.

"Hilma Snapp," she said through gritted teeth.

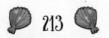

Hilma Snapp smirked. "Where's Zelda and Mimi?"

"Hilma," Beattie pleaded.

"I'VE CAUGHT THE BAD MERMAID!" Hilma roared arrogantly. Beattie turned to see a bunch of Oysterdale mermaids charging toward her, like a tidal wave of bad hats.

"Hilma, this is important," Beattie begged. "We don't have much time before—"

The stadium lights went out.

"Lobstertown is *garbage*," Hilma said, gripping Beattie tighter. "The lights don't even work."

Beyond the railing Beattie could make out a figure swimming onto the track with two glowing crocodile-carved shells strapped to its elbows.

She looked down at Zelda, who was standing next to Liberty Ling!

"Wait," Beattie said frantically. "If Liberty Ling isn't wearing the shells, then that's—"

"Oooh, Ommy Pike!" Hilma oozed, waving madly.

Beattie hastily pulled the shells from her hair. She looked down to see Zelda yanking hers off her wrist.

"Hilma," Beattie said urgently. "Ommy is going to put us all in a trance."

"Well, I've never worn one of those, but I'm sure if Ommy picked it I'll like it."

"Hilma, a trance isn't an outfit. It's *mind control*."

There was a flash of light!

A sickening crack!

And then everything went dark.

31

Disaster

Ommy Pike stood in the royal box, laughing. He had strapped the Ruster Shells to his elbows, the carvings casting crocodile shadows around the stadium.

All the mermaids floated on the spot, their eyes glowing as brightly as the shells.

Beattie swam low, weaving in and out of the mermaids' tails. Her hands were shaking. Everything felt like it was in slow motion—the crowds, the sounds, the huge Clippee cartoon. She collided with Zelda and the pair of them tumbled into a corner of the stadium.

"I WON!" Ommy squealed, trying to kiss the Ruster Shells on his elbows. He snaked toward where Beattie and Zelda were hiding and stopped in front of Liberty Ling. "I CAN'T BELIEVE YOU THOUGHT I WAS GOING TO JUST LET *YOU WEAR* THESE SHELLS? THAT WOULD BE SUCH A WASTE. I CAN CONTROL THE WHOLE LAGOON NOW!"

"Wait," Beattie whispered. "The Swan, Liberty Ling, whatever we call her, she wasn't completely in on it? She didn't know about the put-everyone-in-a-trance plan?"

"AND THE SWAN IS A STUPID NAME!" Ommy shouted in Liberty Ling's face.

She stared at him blankly. Her eyes were glowing.

 217

He turned and inspected the shells on his elbows. "I just needed you for this part of the plan—you're Liberty Ling; you had to be the one to announce the shockey match and get everyone to the stadium without arousing suspicion. Given how much you love collecting shell tops, I knew if I told you I had tracked down the Ruster Shells, convincing you to be part of the plan would be easy. Oh, Arabella Cod will understand once we show her the Ruster Shells, I said. We'll get her back from the human in a few days, I said. Ha!"

Liberty Ling burped.

Beattie watched Riley Ramona and Rachel Rocker sway silently in their shockey gear. Up in the stands, she could see Yule, Malory Swig, and Sabrina Scoosh, all entranced.

"Beatts," Zelda whispered, pointing at the Clippee cartoon. "Look at Steve. He's still going."

Beattie peeked through two mermaid tails and up to the billboard. There Steve was, dancing away as if nothing had happened. "The trance hasn't worked on him, even though he's wearing that shell top."

"Obviously his shell top didn't work," Zelda whispered, "because he's a *sea horse*."

They watched him dance, completely oblivious to what was going on beneath him.

"I can't believe you still have that thing," Zelda said.

Beattie looked from Steve to Ommy and back again. If she could just get Steve to distract him, they could burst out of their hiding place, rip the Ruster Shells from Ommy's elbows, and smash them.

"Psst. Steve!" Beattie tried.

Nothing.

"Clippee, Clippee, Clippee, Clippee, Clippee OH!"

"I'm going to get closer," Beattie said, weaving low through the crowds. "PSST! STEVE!"

A pearly fin dropped down in Beattie's face. Slowly she looked up.

"Well, hello there, little fish," Ommy said with a sinister smile.

"YOU WON'T GET AWAY WITH THIS!" Beattie shouted as she and Ommy spiraled up higher above the entranced mermaid crowd.

"My plan was perfect, even with you little fish trying to meddle with it," Ommy boasted. "You should've seen how I fishnapped Arabella Cod! It involved a trip to Curly Clips and switching places with Liberty Ling at a shockey match!"

"We know," Zelda said grumpily. "Beattie already figured that out."

"And then all I had to do was make sure the palace mermaids were out of the way—we stuffed them in a whale and then stored them somewhere safe. And Arabella Cod was taken to land, where I traded her for the Ruster Shells! An excitable lady with spotted socks had them—she found them on a beach, would you believe?! It's taken me my whole little fishy life to track them down." He cackled as Nom wheeze-laughed next to him.

"Of course," Beattie groaned. "The *pen ink on the crabmail*. That's why she wrote the instructions in pen ink . . . because she was on land, where they use pens."

Zelda flapped her fin angrily. "I can't believe I didn't think of that!"

"So, Ommy, the deal was that you trade Arabella Cod for the Ruster Shells?" Beattie asked.

"Beattie," Zelda pleaded. "Stop talking to it."

Ommy threw his head back and laughed. "That was all I had to do!"

Beattie bit her lip.

"Beatts, what is it?"

"And for the nails, I whipped up some of my special Piranha Powder, a secret recipe of mine. Put it in the Lagoon water, and BOOM, every mermaid had the piranha nails. I smuggled in the piranhas I'd stashed away near Viperview Prison, and voilà! LAGOON CONTROL. Arabella Cod was very impressed when I told her that part of the plan. *Horrified.* But also a bit impressed."

"One more question," Beattie said.

"*Beattie,*" Zelda hissed. "*Don't engage.*"

"Why let the Oysterdale mermaids swim around looting and tell the piranhas to leave them alone, but

then put them in a trance with all the other mermaids anyway?"

"Oh," Ommy said dismissively. "I'm going to base myself in Oysterdale. It's my home, where I grew up. I let them loot as a cheap and effective way of transporting all the good stuff from around the Lagoon to Oysterdale. Now I can move straight in—I have palace treasures, a little shark handbag..."

"EXCUSE YOU! SHARKS ARE NOT FOR HANDBAGS!" came a cry as Steve pelted through the air straight for Ommy! Beattie and Zelda frantically tried to wriggle free.

"Steve!" Beattie cheered, just as Nom appeared behind him.

Zelda screamed as, with one vicious chomp, he bit down hard on Steve.

"NO!" Beattie cried as the wriggling little sea horse went limp and floated down toward the mermaids in a trance below.

"STEVE!" Beattie wailed. "STEVE!" Tears began streaming down her face as she watched Zelda catch him with her tail.

He lay on it, still and quiet: two things that only a dead Steve would be.

Ommy patted Nom. "Well done, my little Nom Nom."

"He was such a lovely little thing," Zelda choked as her eyes welled up with tears.

Steve opened one eye. "I *knew* you liked me."

"Ugh!" Zelda said, flinging him off her tail. "I can't believe you still have that thing, Beattie."

"Steve!" Beattie said, sniffing loudly. "You're alive!"

"But my shell top is ruined," he said angrily, shaking off the broken thing. "It saved my life."

Ommy clenched his fists. "Well, so what? Your sea horse isn't dead. BIG DEAL! You're tied up! What can you possibly do to stop me?"

He cackled.

There was a rumbling sound. Soft at first, then louder and louder.

Ommy peeled the Ruster Shells off his elbows, waved them in the air, and shot up high toward the grand domed roof of the stadium.

"THIS LAGOON IS OFFICIALLY MI—"

A huge shark came crashing through the roof!

"Found it eventually," Mimi said, from where she was sitting on top of it.

Beattie coughed as clouds of sand engulfed the place. When it cleared, she could see a shark flopping where Ommy had just been. A shark covered in fairy lights and a sign that flashed JAWELLA'S.

The lights went back on. The piranhas scattered. The sound of the crowd started up again. The mermaids' eyes stopped glowing.

"Love your work," Mimi said, patting the shark as

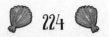

she dismounted it. She swam over to her friends and they linked arms, swimming excitedly in a circle.

"WE DID IT!" Beattie cheered.

"Mimi!" Steve cried, trying to get in the middle of their circle. "You—you completely stole my thunder. I was about to save the day!"

"The piranha marks on my nails have gone!" a mermaid shouted from the crowd.

Beattie looked over at the shark—Ommy was attempting to squeeze his head through the jaws in a bid to escape.

"IT'S SWALLOWED THE RUSTER SHELLS! IT CRUSHED THEM AND SWALLOWED THEM!" he roared.

Zelda rolled back on her tail and folded her arms. "Well, we got there in the end."

"TAKE HIM AWAY!" Beattie ordered as Jawella's slipped back out of the stadium.

"IT'S DISGUSTING IN THIS SHARK!" Ommy cried. "THE FIVE STARFISH ARE A LIE! THE FIVE STARFISH ARE A LIIIIIEEE!"

32

The Palace Mermaids

After the piranhas fled, Silvia Snapp and the Oysterdale mermaids followed. And The Swan, or Liberty Ling, as she really was called, seemed to vanish.

"Leave this to us now," Ray Ramona said, patting Beattie on the shoulder. "We're going to send a search party to land to look for Arabella Cod and the palace mermaids. And we'll see if we can get anything out of Ommy."

"But Ommy said he traded only Arabella Cod. I don't think the palace mermaids are up—"

"Oh, little fish," Goda Gar said, interrupting Beattie. "You go home now. You've done plenty for us, and we are very grateful."

"Well, I'd better get back to Shelly Shelby's Shell Slop," Rachel Rocker said.

"THE SHELLS ARE NO LONGER FREE, YOU

FREELOADERS!" Shelly Shelby roared to any mermaid who would listen.

Riley Ramona swam over. "Let's all go to the Orange Bucket for foam shakes this weekend, now that the cities aren't on lockdown."

"Excellent plan," Rachel Rocker said.

"And, Beattie, bring Steven too!" Riley said.

"Excuse you, it's just *Steve*," Steve said.

Riley and Rachel swam off, out of the giant hole in the stadium roof.

Riley turned back and smiled.

"Riley's teeth actually glint when he smiles," Beattie whispered to Zelda.

Zelda groaned. "Yeah, that's because I knocked some out, remember? He replaced them with some melted-down sunken silver treasure or something. It's tough to find false human teeth down here."

"Well," Beattie said, "if you don't include Steve's bedroom."

Soon everyone was gone, and Beattie floated on the shockey track, the Clippee cartoon still dancing on the board overhead.

The twins were curled up at the side, making Steve a little sandcastle on the sandy stadium floor.

"Excuse you! More turrets."

"Something is wrong," Beattie said. "Ray Ramona is wrong about finding the palace mermaids on land."

"We did it, Beattie," Zelda said as she stuffed Steve in one of the turret windows. "*Relax*. They'll find the palace mermaids."

Beattie shook her head. "No. Ommy said he'd stashed them somewhere safe and THEN he took Arabella Cod to the human on land." Beattie pulled at her plait. "So they must still be somewhere in the Lagoon. And I *bet* wherever they've hidden the palace mermaids and the dolphins was where they hid the Ruster Shells—somewhere secret where no one would see them glow."

"Beattie's right," Mimi said.

Zelda folded her arms. "But where? Where do you

hide over one hundred palace mermaids and some blindingly bright shells?"

Beattie smiled and began drawing a map of the Lagoon on the stadium's sandy floor. North. South. East. West. "Mermaids have been secretly looking for Arabella Cod and the palace mermaids—Rachel Rocker said she sneaked into the palace, and mermaids were looking all over Swirlyshell. Ray Ramona has been looking, and Goda Gar."

"What about Oysterdale?" Mimi suggested. "They were in on it, so it would make sense that they would help Ommy hide them there."

"I thought about that," Beattie said. "But there's nowhere big enough in Oysterdale to stash over a hundred palace mermaids, apart from that theater or Silvia Snapp's sandcastle. But we saw inside both of them, and you destroyed the sandcastle."

Mimi looked guiltily at her hands.

"No," Beattie said confidently. "When Arabella Cod wrote that we were the *only* mermaids who could help, she knew we were the *only* mermaids who could move around the Lagoon freely. And there's only one place where no other mermaids could look. Only one place that isn't a city. Only one place where no mermaids live."

She drew a little ship between Anchor Rock and Lobstertown and looked up at them all.

"But that means—" Steve said slowly.

Beattie nodded. "The *Merry Mary.*"

THE SCRIBBLED SQUID

Sinkers! Eye Mask

Recently been in a trance that made your eyeballs glow? Well then, look no further than the Sinkers! Eye Mask. Made by the Swirlyshell joke shop, this eye mask promises to calm, soothe, and leave a silly squid-ink pattern on your face.

BLINK AND YOU'LL MISS IT! BUY IT NOW!

33

The *Merry Mary* (Oh Cod)

Beattie guided the clam car shakily through the curtain of jellyfish surrounding the *Merry Mary* and parked outside the ancient wreck. The water was cold, and the old masts of the grand ship creaked like they were in some sort of creaking competition.

She tried to block out all the haunted stories about the place that were flooding her mind—the ghosts and ghouls and twisted mermaids—but they kept coming, like a tidal wave that wanted her to turn back.

But she didn't turn back.

Inside, the *Merry Mary* was
all peeling wallpaper and
creaking furniture.

On a desk Beattie saw piles of fresh seaweed slips covered in doodles for a magnificent display cabinet.

"Look at that," Beattie said. She swam over to the desk. "It says 'The Swan's Shell Top Collection'! Liberty Ling didn't want to put everyone in a trance. She just really liked shell tops. Look, she's also got a cabinet for her collection of dried shrimp in hats.

"MELP, MET US MOUT!" came cries from the next room. The double doors had been nailed shut with piranha teeth.

"Quick!" Beattie said, grabbing the desk.

"I'll just fin-fu chop the doors," Mimi said casually, inspecting her nails.

"NO!" Beattie and Zelda cried at once.

"We don't want another Smug Street castle scenario while we're *inside* the ship, thank you, Mimi," Zelda said, rolling her eyes.

"As you wish," Mimi said with a shrug, floating over to help them move the desk. Steve sat on the desk, directing them.

"Excuse you! Left. *Left*."

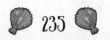

They aligned it perfectly with the double doors.

"Ready?" Beattie said.

"ALWAYS!" Zelda roared, pushing the desk forward. It crashed through the doors, sending glamorous palace mermaids spilling out. They were all sporting pearly outfits and matching white hair pulled into sculpted shell shapes.

"Well done, little fish!" Mimi and Zelda's mom cheered, her dark purple lipstick slightly smudged around the edges.

The twins' dad wore oversized round glasses that rocked precariously on his bulbous nose. "You little mermaids did great!"

"Beattie figured out you were here," Zelda said proudly.

The palace mermaids hoisted Beattie up and clapped, slapping their tails on the ship's old wooden floor.

"Bea-ttie! Bea-ttie! Bea-ttie!" Steve shouted, trying to get a chant going, but the palace mermaids weren't paying attention.

Mimi wrenched open a large cupboard and two furious-looking dolphins shot out— and straight through one of the ship's portholes, the glass shattering loudly as they did so.

"Arabella Cod's dolphins," the twins' dad said knowingly. "I wouldn't like to be the human who's keeping her captive on land . . ."

"So they must've stashed Arabella Cod here too, before they transported her to land," Beattie mused. "Liberty Ling met her just outside Lobstertown, then I bet she lured her here somehow."

"She probably used the same tactic she used to get us in the whale," the twins' mom said.

"What was that?" Mimi asked.

"Oh, she said she'd met a ghost named Carl by the ship. It sounds silly, but we were all very excited!"

"Very sad he wasn't real," said a tiny palace mermaid with sagging earlobes. "Very sad."

As the palace mermaids soared off in their incredible shell-covered carriages, Beattie, Mimi, Zelda, and Steve sat on the roof of the clam car staring out at the Swirlyshell spires glinting in the distance.

There wasn't a sinister cloud of squid ink or a piranha in sight.

"*This* is more like it," Beattie said with a sigh.

Zelda put her arms around Beattie and Mimi. "I'M ONE HAPPY HOT DOG!" she shouted, making them all snort-laugh.

34

BUT...

They all climbed into the Clamorado 7.

"We'd better return this to the Snapps now," Beattie said, just as there was a crash from inside the *Merry Mary*.

They all looked at each other.

"It's probably just a jellyfish," Zelda said.

"Or a *ghost*," Mimi whispered.

"There's not really much difference between a jellyfish and a ghost, appearance-wise, is there?" Steve mused.

Beattie couldn't resist. "I'll just be a second." She swam back into the *Merry Mary*, her heart pounding.

"She just can't resist," Zelda said. "Like mother, like daughter."

Steve followed, then Mimi.

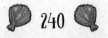

"Oh, can't we just go *home*? Ghosts aren't *real*!" Zelda called after them. She waited on her own for a moment. A jellyfish wafted past her left cheek, making her scream.

"WAIT FOR ME!" she wailed, bursting through the *Merry Mary*'s crumbling door.

The four of them floated nervously, staring at the cupboard. Inside, they could hear movement. Banging. A weird sort-of squeak.

"HELLO?" Mimi shouted.

"Mimi," Beattie hissed as Steve dived into the false teeth in her hand.

Zelda floated at a safe distance, all the way across the other side of the room.

Beattie was sure she could hear grunting coming from inside. "What's *in* there?" she whispered.

"I'll ask," Mimi said, casually throwing the door open.

Beattie winced and dived out of the way. But there was no need. Standing in front of them in her ridiculous hat and suit of smugness was *Hilma Snapp*.

She glared at them. "What? So I thought I'd see what you were all doing . . . and then I got *stuck*."

"I wonder what this does?!" Zelda called over from the other side of the room. She was pointing at a small shell button.

Mimi's eyes widened.

"Zelda," Beattie said, approaching slowly. "Don—"

But it was too late.

She pressed it.

The ship began to rock.

Lights flickered.

Beattie looked out the window—an old steel-pipe entrance opened up, just like the one they'd used to sneak into the Lagoon!

Zelda and Mimi held on to the walls as the boat began to move.

"SOMEONE STOP IT!" Hilma screamed as Beattie tore across to the opposite window and peered out.

The spires of Swirlyshell vanished as the ship swirled and squeezed through the pipe, up and out, soaring fast through the mysterious waters of the Upper Realm.

Steve peeked out of his false teeth. "Oh, this is *bad*."

CLAMZINE

MISSING IN THE UPPER REALMS!

Beattie Shelton, Mimi and Zelda Swish, Hilma Snapp, the *Merry Mary*, and a talking sea horse who responds to "Steve."

If found, please return to the Hidden Lagoon near the NO LEGS BEYOND THIS POINT sign. Please drop off at Periwinkle Palace, Swirlyshell.

Password: Ihavenolegs.

BEATTIE

MIMI   ZELDA

STEVE

Hilma Snapp

Merry Mary

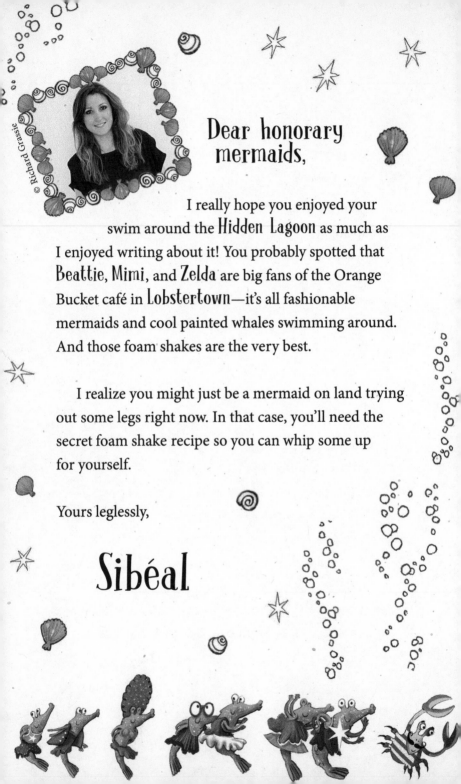

© Richard Grassie

Dear honorary mermaids,

I really hope you enjoyed your swim around the **Hidden Lagoon** as much as I enjoyed writing about it! You probably spotted that **Beattie, Mimi,** and **Zelda** are big fans of the Orange Bucket café in **Lobstertown**—it's all fashionable mermaids and cool painted whales swimming around. And those foam shakes are the very best.

I realize you might just be a mermaid on land trying out some legs right now. In that case, you'll need the secret foam shake recipe so you can whip some up for yourself.

Yours leglessly,

Sibéal

Orange Bucket Foam Shakes

You'll need (to make four foam shakes):

✳ 4 cups milk (or a substitute)

✳ ¼ cup sugar

✳ 1½ teaspoons pure vanilla extract

✳ Caramel drizzle (human supermarkets sell this caramel stuff in squeeze bottles, or you can make your own from scratch)

✳ Orange sprinkles

1. Simmer the milk and sugar in a saucepan (get an adult human to do the hard work for you), stirring until the sugar is dissolved.

2. Stir in the vanilla extract.

3. Pour into four mugs. When on land, mermaids like to drink foam shakes secretly out of cool tin mugs. But you can use any mug, or a drinking shell.

4. Drizzle the caramel over the top and add the orange sprinkles.

5. Let it cool a little and enjoy! It'll be just like you're deep underwater at the Orange Bucket in Lobstertown.

Sibéal Pounder is the author of the Witch Wars series. She has written for publications including the *Guardian*, fashion-trend forecaster WGSN, Vogue.com, and the *Financial Times*, where she was the resident philanthropy columnist for the How to Spend It section for four years—interviewing everyone from Vivienne Westwood to Veronica Etro.

www.sibealpounder.com

@sibealpounder

Jason Cockcroft graduated from Falmouth School of Art in 1994 and has been working as an illustrator of children's books ever since. He won the Blue Peter Book Award for his work on Geraldine McCaughrean's retelling of *A Pilgrim's Progress* and was the illustrator on the original covers of the final three Harry Potter novels.

jasoncockcroft.co.uk